The Newspaper Kids 4

Spooking Sally

First published in Australia by **Angus&Robertson** in 1996
An imprint of HarperCollins*Publishers*, Australia
First published in Great Britain by Collins 1999
Collins is an imprint of HarperCollins*Publishers* Ltd,
77-85 Fulham Palace Road, Hammersmith, London W6 8JB

The HarperCollins website address is www.**fire**and**water**.com

3 5 7 9 8 6 4 2

Text copyright © Juanita Phillips 1996

ISBN 0 00 675463 5

The author asserts the moral right to be identified as author of the work

Printed and bound in Great Britain by
Omnia Books Limited, Glasgow

The Newspaper Kids 4

Spooking Sally

Juanita Phillips

Illustrations by Mark David

Collins

An Imprint of HarperCollins*Publishers*

Meet The Newspaper Kids

Hugo

Jasper and I are so close in age we are almost twins but, unlike me, my older sister can be a pain — she's always grabbing the good things for herself. So when it came to giving ourselves jobs on our newspaper, no one was more surprised than me to be given the job of chief reporter.

Chasing criminals and solving mysteries was what I'd always wanted to do, but chief reporter? That sounded important . . . and, what's even better, fun!

Jasper

Thank goodness, Hugo agreed to be chief reporter because while he's chasing criminals, someone has to interview the famous people . . . and that leaves me! It won't be easy — being glamorous is hard work. Most importantly, the kids of Blue Rock need a voice and mine's the loudest.

Everyone has a right to be heard; especially kids, and especially me!

Frankie

A reporter could have the best story in Blue Rock, an exclusive, but without a picture, the reporter has no proof. Luckily my nose for trouble and my eye for detail leads me and my cameras to be in the right place at the right time and SNAP! Instant evidence.

A picture speaks a thousand words, as my dad used to say, so when someone says — get the picture? I do!

Toby

Putting together a newspaper is a bit like putting together a jigsaw. And to put together a good newspaper, you need a lot of pieces.

That's why I am lucky to have Frankie's photographs and reporters like my best friend Jasper, and her brother, Hugo. What Jasper doesn't know, Hugo is sure to find out!

If a story breaks . . . the newspaper kids are on the case!

*For Lindy, Bigz and Joey Budd — Brisbane's
original newspaper kids ~ J. P.*

Chapter One

'The age of the dinosaurs began two hundred and twenty-five million years ago,' droned the small, bearded man at the front of the classroom. 'One of the fiercest creatures to roam the southern lands of the planet was the Great Scaly Ockersaurus. Does anyone know what Ockersaurus means?'

'Tiny brain,' I mumbled, staring out the window.

'Tiny brain,' murmured the rest of the class.

We all liked dinosaurs but this was baby stuff. Any minute now, this crusty old professor would probably be telling us that the Tyrannosaurus rex was the biggest dinosaur of all time. How old did he think we were? Three?

'Correct.' The professor whipped the monocle from his eye, breathed on it, then polished it briskly with a crisp white handkerchief. Everything he did was snappy, like a robot.

He replaced the monocle and peered at us haughtily. 'The Ockersaurus was large, aggressive, but extremely stupid. Experts such as myself have little doubt that its tiny brain was the reason for its eventual extinction.'

Bored, I scrunched up a piece of paper into a ball and looked around the room for my big sister Jasper, so I could throw it at her. She is a year older than me, but today Grades Five and Six were mixed in together to listen to this special talk.

Ever since some rare dinosaur bones had been dug up in Blue Rock's park two weeks before, our town had been crawling with experts — and Professor Maxwell Wally, with his little pointed beard waggling as he talked, was one of them. He'd come all the way from America to study Blue Rock's own special dinosaur.

The dinosaur's official name was Great Scaly Ockersaurus, but the town called him Neville after Nev the 'Rev-Head' Reilly, who found the bones while churning up the ground in his hotted-up car one night. Neville was the only perfectly intact Ockersaurus skeleton in the world. He'd been quietly fossilising for more than two hundred million years,

but since he was dug up he'd become a world-famous celebrity. Neville was the biggest thing to happen to Blue Rock in . . . well, in two hundred million years! But this professor was starting to get a bit boring.

A movement at the back of the class caught my eye. It was Howard Fitzherbert, the school bully. He wasn't listening to the professor either. He had something in his hands that he was fidgeting with. I looked closer. It was a glass jar. And inside, was the biggest, brownest bush spider I'd ever seen in my life.

It was a whopper.

I forgot about paper-bombing Jasper and watched, fascinated, as Howard turned the jar around and gently tapped on the glass. Howard was concentrating so hard on this spider that I could see his tongue poking out the corner of his mouth. Slowly and carefully, he unscrewed the lid of the jar and lifted it off. I heard somebody gasp softly and realised that everyone else in the classroom was watching Howard and the spider, too. Everyone, that is, except two people: Professor Wally, and the girl sitting right in front of Howard. The new girl. Sally Champion.

As the professor drivelled on, I watched Howard lift the glass jar over Sally Champion's head. By now, the new girl was the only one in the classroom listening to the professor talk about dinosaurs. She had her back to Howard, and was too busy taking notes to realise that everyone else had their attention focused on her.

With an evil smile, Howard held the open jar over Sally's head. I could see the spider waving its long hairy legs. It started to move towards the top of the jar, and freedom. A wave of dizziness swept over me and I realised I'd been holding my breath. Now that the spider was on the move, I could see it was as big as my hand.

I tried to call out to Sally to warn her, but my voice had dried up, and all that came out was a frightened croak.

Slowly, with a menacing leer, Howard tilted the glass jar. The giant brown spider hesitated for a moment, then crawled out ... straight onto Sally Champion's shiny black hair.

Somebody moaned softly. With a start, I realised it was me. The professor's voice was now just a low buzz in the background. All I could see was the world's biggest brown bush spider sitting on Sally Champion's head. Everything else was a blur. And Sally? She just kept writing notes as though nothing had happened.

Suddenly, the spider started crawling over Sally's hair towards her face. I closed my eyes, waiting for the screams. But they didn't come.

When I opened my eyes, Sally Champion was casually holding the world's biggest brownest bush

spider in her hand, and looking at it with interest.

Then she turned around to face Howard Fitzherbert, looked him straight in the eye, and popped the spider in her mouth.

Somebody screamed. Two of the girls started bawling and one of the boys dived under his desk. The professor stopped talking. Everybody — including Howard Fitzherbert — stared open-mouthed as Sally Champion crunched up that spider. Sally chewed for a few seconds, then swallowed.

Then she smiled, and rubbed her stomach.

'Mmmm,' said Sally Champion. 'Tastes like . . . chicken.'

'She's nuts,' announced Jasper, flopping into one of the Cave's old couches. 'Mad as a meat-axe. Crazy as a cut snake. Loopy as a loon.'

It was two hours later, and we were sitting in the old shed we used as a newspaper office — the Cave — trying to come up with ideas for the next edition of *Street Wise*. But somehow the conversation kept coming back to Sally Champion.

'She must be a fruit cake,' added my best friend Frankie, who was cleaning her camera lenses. 'Did you see the way she just crammed that spider into her mouth? I was scared to death just watching her.'

I shuddered, and said nothing. Up until two hours

ago, I hadn't even realised I had a terrible fear of spiders. Our friend Toby — the smartest kid in Blue Rock and the editor of *Street Wise* — had looked it up in the medical dictionary. Arachnophobia, they called it. Apparently you couldn't die from it, but the way I felt now, I wasn't so sure.

My dog Scoop — the newspaper's mascot and Great Fierce Guardian of the Cave — nuzzled my hand, sensing that something was wrong. But even patting him didn't make me feel any better. Stroking his smooth black coat reminded me of the spider's hairy legs . . .

I felt another wave of anxiety coming, and reached for the chocolate biscuits. I'd discovered from past experience that chocolate was an excellent treatment for shock. But I'd already eaten half a packet of biscuits, and it hadn't made much difference at all. Every time I crunched into one, I thought about Sally Champion, crunching on the spider. Its legs reminded me of crispy, fried brown noodles . . .

'Stop thinking about it, Hugo,' ordered Toby. 'Like any phobia, a fear of spiders is all in the mind. Concentrate on something else . . . like *Street Wise*.' He tapped the computer screen with a worried expression on his face. 'The dinosaur discovery is the big news of course, but the *Blue Rock Bugle*'s already done it to death. We need something else . . . something different.'

'Well, I've already done my celebrity interview,' announced Jasper smugly. 'Professor Wally! I spoke to him exclusively after school today. *Street Wise*'s first foreign celebrity! He told me everything, and believe me, he didn't hold anything back . . .'

While Jasper raved on, I took a deep breath and looked around the Cave trying to take my mind off the spider. There was something very comforting about being here. To most people, it probably just looked like a shabby old shed that had once been a garage, but to us, it was our special place — the place where we came up with our best ideas, and turned them into an eight-page newspaper for kids. Maybe Toby was right. If I didn't think about the spider, it was almost as though it didn't exist.

'You know, I think that girl Sally is the bravest girl I've ever seen,' said Frankie thoughtfully. She hadn't heard a word Jasper had been saying. 'She looks like nothing scares her at all.'

Jasper sat up crossly and flicked her long orange plaits behind her shoulders. 'Rubbish. Everyone's scared of *something*. Even grown-ups.' She looked at Toby. 'Well? Am I right?'

Toby nodded. 'Affirmative. Fear is necessary for survival. If we didn't feel fear, we wouldn't know

when to run from danger. Everybody feels fear —
it's part of being human.'

I hadn't thought of it that way. My fear of spiders
didn't sound like such a disaster after all. 'So what
are you scared of?' I asked Toby curiously.

He blushed and pushed his thick spectacles more
firmly onto his nose. 'Well, this sounds a bit silly . . .
but I'm scared of the dark. That's why I keep a
night-light on. I used to think there were monsters
under my bed when I was little.'

'Me, I'm terrified of heights.' Frankie snapped the
lens back onto her camera and peered through the
viewfinder to check it. 'Petrified of them. My dad
was the same. If I'm in a tall building and I look out
the window . . . YIKES! I get all dizzy and feel like
I'm going to fall over. They call it vertigo.'

'That's nothing,' interrupted Jasper, trying to steal
the limelight as usual. 'My fear's much worse than
any of those.'

I waited expectantly. I reckoned Jasper's biggest
fear in life would be having a gag in her mouth so
she couldn't talk.

'The — sight — of — blood.' Jasper paused
dramatically. 'When I did that first aid course, I was
so scared I fainted.' She looked around at us
triumphantly. 'And that was *fake* blood they used.
That's how scared I was.'

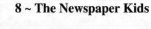

Toby coughed politely. 'Well, that's very impressive, Jasper. But I really think we should get back to *Street Wise*. We're getting very close to deadline and . . .'

He stopped, his voice suddenly drowned out by a loud, grating noise coming from outside.

Scoop pricked up his ears, growling.

Ker-chunk. Ker-chunk. It sounded like a skateboard coming down the rough concrete driveway that led from Toby's front gate all the way to the Cave. A skateboard going very, very fast.

I rushed to the window and looked out. It *was* a skateboard coming down the concrete path. It was going a million miles an hour and it was heading straight for the Cave.

And riding it, dressed in a cowgirl outfit, with her dead-straight black hair streaming out behind her, was Sally Champion.

'Gosh, I'm starving.'

Sally walked through the door of the Cave as though she owned it.

The four of us stared at her, speechless. Scoop stopped growling. He seemed to have forgotten he was the Great Fierce Guardian of the Cave. He just stood there with his head cocked to one side looking as confused as the rest of us.

'You're hungry?' said Jasper sarcastically, finally finding her voice. 'I thought you'd already eaten.'

I watched as Sally walked over to the chocolate biscuits, bold as brass, and took one. I was still trying to work out how she flipped the skateboard up and caught it just millimetres before she crashed into the wall.

'You mean the spider? I didn't really eat it.' Sally smiled, revealing a set of bright pink and green braces on her teeth. 'I only pretended. It's called sleight of hand. I learned it from a book, when I was going to be a magician.' She paused. 'Decades ago. Before I decided to be an explorer instead.'

I gulped. 'But I saw you . . .'

Sally reached into her pocket and drew out a small drawstring bag made of brown suede. 'She's in here, if you don't believe me. Her name's Amelia. Amelia the Huntsman. She's quite tame.'

I jumped back, alarmed. 'You've got the spider in *that*?'

Sally Champion finished the biscuit and daintily replaced the bag in her pocket before she replied. 'Only until I finish building her new home. I've got this old glass aquarium that I'm going to build a make-believe miniature forest in. That way I can watch Amelia spin a web before I let her go.'

Toby cleared his throat nervously. 'Sally, how come you always wear that Western outfit?'

Sally was dressed from head to foot like something out of the Wild West — caramel-coloured fringed vest with matching pants, and real leather cowboy boots with steel caps and silver spurs. She smoothed the leather fringing on her soft suede vest. 'It's supremely cool, isn't it? Just like the ones the cowboys wear in Vietnam. That's where I come from, you know. At least my mum does. There are heaps of cowboys there. The ranches are crawling with them.'

I frowned, trying to remember what I'd learned about Vietnam at school. I couldn't remember much about cowboys.

'I thought Vietnam was mostly rice paddies,' I said doubtfully.

'Sure. Heaps of rice paddies. That's so they can feed the cowboys' horses.' Sally grinned wickedly. 'Of course, I could just be pulling your leg.'

I looked at her, dumbfounded. Was she serious? Or just nuts, like Jasper had said? And what on earth was she doing here? Nobody — *nobody* — came into the Cave without an invitation.

'I think what you did this afternoon was pretty brave,' said Frankie. 'I just wish I'd had my camera there to take a photo of Howard Fitzherbert's face.'

'Well, I don't think it was brave,' snapped Jasper,

stepping forward with her hands on her hips. She put her face about ten centimetres away from Sally's and glared at her. 'I think it was stupid. And anyway, you're not an explorer.'

Sally didn't flinch. In fact, she pushed her face even closer to Jasper's — and smiled. 'Not yet I'm not,' she said calmly. 'But when I grow up I will be.'

Jasper stepped back. I could tell the smile had caught her off-guard. Usually when old Barracuda Brain decides to freeze someone out, they get the message quick smart. But Sally didn't even seem to notice.

'There's no such thing as explorers anyway,' continued Jasper crossly. But she didn't sound so certain any more. 'Everything's been discovered. You won't be able to get a job. There's nowhere on earth left to explore.'

She was right — but somehow I didn't think Sally Champion was ready to surrender.

'Oh, I'm not talking about exploring the earth,' said Sally, waving her hand dismissively. 'I'm talking about *space*.'

This was getting stranger by the second. A skateboarding, spider-wrangling, space exploring cowgirl?

There was no doubt about it. Between the dinosaur and Sally Champion, I had a hunch that life in Blue Rock was about to get very, very interesting.

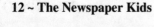

Chapter Two

Yep, Sally was a weirdo all right — the spider episode proved that — but there was something cool about her, too. Maybe it was the pink and green braces. Or the fact that Scoop liked her straight away. Or maybe it was the brave way she just turned up at the Cave that day uninvited — and announced that she was joining our newspaper.

'You're doing WHAT!' shrieked Jasper.

'I — I beg your pardon?' stuttered Toby at the same time, his glasses sliding right off the end of his nose with shock.

Frankie and I nudged each other. This was getting interesting.

The new girl perched herself on the arm of the old couch and nodded energetically. 'I've put a lot of thought into it, and I've decided it's a good thing for all of us.'

'How do you figure that?' I asked faintly. I'd never met anyone as bold as Sally Champion in my life. She didn't even seem to notice that Jasper's face was turning purple with rage — or if she did, it didn't bother her.

'Yes, do tell us,' said Jasper between gritted teeth. 'Seeing as how you don't even *know* us.'

'Well, it's good for me because I need the training. If I'm going to be an explorer I need to have a few adventures — and reporters have plenty of those,' explained Sally confidently, ignoring Jasper's icy tone.

I watched, dismayed, as she helped herself to the last biscuit.

'And it's good for *you* because I'd be such a fantastic reporter,' continued Sally, breaking the biscuit in two and giving half to Scoop. 'I'm not scared of anything. You could send me on any assignment, any time . . .'

'Stop — right — there.' Toby picked his glasses up off the floor and settled them firmly onto his nose again. 'I'm sure you'd be very good, Sally, but the fact is we're not hiring at the moment. You have to understand there are lots of kids who want to become reporters for *Street Wise* . . .'

'But I'm different,' stated Sally matter-of-factly. 'Like I said, I'm not scared of anything. I'll prove it to you if you like.'

The skateboarding cowgirl just didn't get the hint.

'You're taking up valuable real estate,' snapped Jasper. 'Maybe you'd better catch the next air current out of here.'

'No offence,' I added, trying to take the sting out of Jasper's words. 'It's just that the four of us started *Street Wise* and . . .'

Sally held her hands up in the 'surrender' position. 'And you don't want any newcomers barging in. I understand.'

The four of us breathed a sigh of relief. It seemed like the new girl had finally got the message.

Sally got up to leave, her silver spurs tinkling like Christmas bells. But as she reached the door, she stopped, and turned around.

'If you change your mind, the offer's still open.' She flashed her pink and green braces at us. 'Never say never, that's my motto . . .'

Before we could tell her to forget it, Sally Champion had jumped on her skateboard and was gone.

'That girl's so full of herself, she's likely to explode,' muttered Jasper. 'What a cheek! Wasting our time like that . . .' She glared at Scoop. 'Fat lot of good you were. Some guardian!'

Scoop slunk under the couch, licking the final biscuit crumbs from his whiskers.

Toby was gazing into the computer screen thoughtfully. 'I'm not so sure it was a waste of time. Something Sally said has given me a good idea.'

I closed the door to the Cave and locked it, to make sure there'd be no other interruptions. 'You're not going to hire her, are you?'

Toby shook his head. 'No. But she could be the answer to our circulation problems.'

We stared at him, mystified. Our dropping circulation was a touchy subject. Usually, we sold about eighty-five copies of *Street Wise* a month — especially when we had a good story on the front page. But lately, that had dropped to about sixty copies. Now that the novelty of a kids' newspaper was wearing off, a lot of our readers were getting lazy. They'd buy one copy and pass it among four or five of them to save money. Or they'd borrow it from the school library. More and more people were reading our paper, but our profits were dropping. We were always looking for ways to boost our sales — but Sally Champion? What was Toby on about?

'Look at the *Blue Rock Bugle*.' Toby tossed a copy of the local grown-up's paper on the desk.

'Circulation's up by twenty percent. Hundreds of extra people are reading it. And guess what the reason is?'

I racked my brains. 'They're giving it away for nothing?'

Toby frowned. 'The reason they're selling more papers is this.' He pointed to a headline on the front page. 'Bingo. Blue Rock Bingo. It's a competition.'

'So?' I shrugged. 'The *Bugle*'s giving away a thousand dollars a day. Of course people buy the paper if they think they can win it. But we can't offer a prize like that.'

'It's not just the money.' Toby paced the room, his eyes shining. 'It's the challenge. People love to win. *That's* why they buy the *Bugle* . . . because it's fun to enter the competition!'

Jasper sighed impatiently. 'So, what's your point, Toby? What's Sally Champion got to do with Blue Rock Bingo?'

Suddenly, Frankie spoke up from the corner where she'd been sitting quietly, fiddling with her cameras. 'Toby thinks we need a competition in *Street Wise*. To get kids to buy it. To lift our circulation.'

Toby bowed in her direction. 'Thank you, Francesca. You read my mind.'

I still didn't get it. 'And Sally Champion . . . ?'

Toby smiled secretively and blinked at me through his thick glasses.

'Oh, she's very important. You see, brave Sally *is* our competition.'

He fixed me with a purposeful stare. I knew that look. It was the look Toby got whenever he was about to give me a big assignment.

'Sally Champion is going to help us double our circulation,' declared the editor of *Street Wise*. 'And you, Hugo, are going to convince her of that.'

'She'll never do it,' I grumbled as Frankie, Scoop and I made our way to the Blue Rock Shopping Centre after school the next day.

Frankie shrugged. 'You'll never know unless you try. After all, she can only say no.'

'Of course she'll say no,' I said gloomily. 'Who in their right mind would agree to a hare-brained scheme like this?'

The Spooking Sally Challenge. I repeated the words in my mind for the hundredth time. I had to admit — if we managed to pull it off, it would be the most exciting competition Blue Rock had ever seen. As Toby explained it, the idea was to try to scare Sally, the bravest girl in Blue Rock. We'd ask the readers of *Street Wise* to submit their ideas on how to 'spook' Sally. The suggestions could be as bizarre and as silly as they liked. There were only two condition: the scary dares had to be legal, and safe.

'For example, we couldn't ask Sally to jump off a cliff,' Toby had said. 'That wouldn't be brave — it'd just be stupid. But we could — for example — blindfold her, and get her to go on the Flying Fox without telling her what it was.'

I thought about it as the three of us crossed the carpark in front of the shopping centre. The Flying Fox was just about the scariest thing in Blue Rock, and the thought of somebody going on it blindfolded sent a shiver down my spine.

'Nobody in their right mind,' I repeated, 'would volunteer for something like this.'

Frankie turned to me and grinned.

'We're talking about Sally Champion, Hugo,' she said. 'She might just be crazy enough to say yes.'

The Champions ran the Great Buns! bakery in the shopping centre. Sally's parents had bought it when they moved to Blue Rock a few months earlier. I knew that Sally went there every day after she'd picked her little sister Milly up from kindergarten.

Dogs weren't allowed inside, so I tied Scoop up and told him to wait for us. I had a feeling we wouldn't be long. Sally would probably laugh us right out the door when she heard our idea.

When we got to Great Buns! Mrs Champion was serving customers and I could see Sally sitting at a tiny table in the kitchen area out the back doing her homework. I wondered how on earth she could concentrate with so much noise going on, and with Milly playing right next to her.

'Hey! What are you two doing here?' Sally's face lit up when she saw us. Even from that distance I could see her bright pink and green braces. 'Come out the back! Dad's just made some pastries.'

I looked around in awe. I'd never been in a bakery before. It was hot and noisy, and it smelled delicious.

'Who's that?' I whispered, as a big, pink-faced man in a white apron and cap waved cheerfully at us.

'My dad. He makes all this stuff.' Sally gestured casually at row upon row of gleaming stainless steel trolleys, stacked with bread and cakes. She pointed to a thin, dark-haired man who was kneading dough. 'That's my Uncle Tan. He lives with us, too, with Auntie Lee and their new baby.'

She grabbed a handful of steaming pastries studded with currants, and thrust them at us. 'Be careful. They're hot.'

I watched Sally closely as I bit into the pastry. She didn't seem angry at us — quite the opposite, in fact. Maybe she'd forgotten how we hadn't exactly welcomed her with open arms to the Cave yesterday.

Sally saw me looking at her. 'Come on, I'll show you around.'

I swallowed the last bit of pastry, and looked nervously at Frankie. 'Actually, Sally, we've come to talk to you. About the newspaper.'

Sally clapped her hands. 'I knew it! You've changed your minds!'

'Er . . . not exactly.' I took a deep breath and told Sally our proposal. How we had chosen her to be the star of the world's most amazing and exciting competition: the Spooking Sally Challenge. How she could put her courage to the test in a dare 'n' scare extravaganza that would go down in the history books of Blue Rock. How huge crowds would gather as news of the competition spread via the Internet.

The more I told her, the sillier it sounded. Any faint hope I had of talking Sally into this ludicrous scheme was fading fast, and I started to wonder what on earth I was doing here. Sally just listened to me rabbiting on with an amused expression on her face.

'After all, you did offer to prove your courage to us,' I concluded in a rush, adding lamely, 'and it would really help our circulation.'

Sally leaned back against the wall and folded her arms. 'Spooking Sally, huh? So what's in it for me?'

I hesitated. That was something I hadn't thought about.

Frankie saw my dilemma, and jumped in. 'Well, you'd meet a lot of new people,' she said brightly. 'And you'd become really famous. I'll be photographing all your dares, of course, and the pictures will be published in *Street Wise*.'

Sally smiled regretfully and shook her head. 'Thanks, but I already meet a lot of people here at Great Buns!,' she said. 'And I'm not interested in fame.'

So I'd been right. There was no way anybody — even a crazy skateboarding cowgirl — would agree to be the main stooge in a daredevil contest.

'But I'll tell you what,' said Sally Champion, regarding us with her calm hazel eyes, 'I'll make a deal with you.'

My heart skipped a beat. Maybe . . . maybe I was wrong.

'I'll agree to the Spooking Sally Challenge,' Sally said slowly, 'on one condition.'

Yikes! A condition? This was something I hadn't bargained on.

'What's the condition?' I said warily.

'The condition is this,' said Sally Champion. 'If I win the challenge — if nobody finds a way to scare me — then I get a job as a reporter on *Street Wise*.'

In the stunned silence that followed, Mrs Champion's voice suddenly rang out.

'Sally! Come and help me serve!'

Sally stood there calmly as if she hadn't heard. 'That's the deal. If you can't scare me — I get the job. Take it or leave it. Your choice.'

Some choice! My head ached with the decision we were being forced to make. If only Toby and Jasper were here, too. If only we had more time . . .

'Sal! You heard your mum!' It was Mr Champion this time, sounding impatient. 'Hop out there and give her a hand, love.'

It looked like it was now or never. If I waited to talk to the others about it, Sally could change her mind and withdraw her offer completely.

Frantically, I weighed up the odds. If Sally won the Challenge, she'd get a job on *Street Wise* — and the others would kill me.

On the other hand, what were the chances that Sally Champion could perform every terrifying dare that was put to her, and not be scared of one of them?

'Everybody's scared of something,' Toby had said. *'It's part of being human.'*

Sally was human — therefore she had to be scared of something. All we had to do was find out what it was. It might be hard — but surely it wasn't impossible.

I stuck out my hand.

'It's a deal,' I told Sally. 'Let's shake on it.'

Chapter Three

The crowd in front of the museum doors was enormous, and it was growing bigger by the second.

Squashed in the middle of it, surrounded by the entire population of our school, I wondered if I'd make it into the museum alive. My face was pressed against Howard Fitzherbert's back, and with a hundred other kids pushing me from behind, I could hardly breathe — let alone move. Today was the first day Blue Rock's famous Ockersaurus had gone on public display — but at this rate, I was going to be trampled to death before I even got a glimpse of him.

'Watch it, moron,' snarled Howard, looking over his shoulder. 'Stop pushing!'

'I'm not!' I gasped. I was running out of fresh air fast and the only solution I could think of was a snorkel.

'Hugo! Over here!' Someone was yelling out my name. Pinned against Howard, the best I could do was swivel my eyes. I saw Toby a few metres away, with Jasper next to him, waving madly at me. Toby was holding up a thick wad of paper in the air. 'The leaflets! The Spooking Sally leaflets! I've done them!'

The leaflets? Already? Boy, was I in trouble. Toby had come up with the idea of the leaflets yesterday, after I told him that Sally had agreed to be in the Challenge. He thought it would be the best way to let people know about it.

The only problem was, I didn't get round to telling him the *other* side of the bargain — the bit about Sally becoming a reporter for *Street Wise* if we couldn't come up with a way to scare her. Okay, so it was a pretty important bit — but somehow it just slipped my mind at the time. I'd been planning to break the news to Toby today, after the dinosaur excursion, and suggest we call the whole thing off. But now he'd gone and printed the leaflets, and if I didn't do something it would be too late.

I had to stop him handing them out.

'Excuse me! Let me through! Please!' Panting, I tried to push my way through the crowd to reach

Toby. It was almost impossible. Kids were packed as tight as sardines, all wanting to be first through the museum doors when they opened.

Desperately, I scanned the crowd for Frankie. Maybe she could help. But just as I spotted her — up a nearby tree snapping photographs of the scene — somebody handed me a piece of paper. I looked at it and groaned. It was a Spooking Sally leaflet — and everybody else had one, too.

Suddenly the crowd surged forward, taking me with it.

'We want to see the dinosaur!' shouted someone. 'We want to see Neville!'

The mob took up the chant. 'Nev-ILLE! Nev-ILLE!' The kids at the front started pounding on the doors.

It looked like there'd be a full-on riot unless somebody opened the museum doors quick smart. The teachers were running around like sheepdogs yapping at everyone to settle down, but it didn't do much good. The excitement of seeing the Ockersaurus for the first time was building to fever-pitch — and troubled as I was by my guilty secret, I couldn't help but get swept along with it.

'Move it!' barked a familiar voice. 'Out of my way!' It was Marilyn Miller, the TV reporter with brassy yellow hair and shoulder pads big enough to break rocks. She was forcing a path through the crowd, with a cameraman and a sound assistant struggling along behind her lugging all the equipment.

'TV crew coming through!' yelled Marilyn importantly. She swung her handbag around her head like a Viking going into battle. 'We have an exclusive on this story. Nobody sees the dinosaur until we've finished filming!'

A mutinous mumble rippled through the crowd. It didn't seem fair. After all, we'd been waiting for hours.

Marilyn's handbag whacked me in the jaw as she pushed past. 'Watch out, boy!' she snapped. 'You'll smudge my make-up.'

Marilyn's manners weren't very good — but she certainly got results. No sooner had she rapped on the doors waving her press pass, than they magically opened. The museum's curator, Mrs Bottomley, took one look at the pushing, shoving mass of kids behind Marilyn, and tried to shut the doors in a big hurry.

But she was too late. Unstoppable as a tidal wave, we were already inside, pounding down the corridors hot on the tail of the TV crew.

Mrs Bottomley trailed behind, flapping her arms and squawking in outrage.

'Stop! Stop! The museum isn't open yet . . .'

Nobody took the slightest bit of notice.

Hooting with excitement, we stampeded through the museum towards the palaeontology section. For the moment, I'd completely forgotten about the mess I was in with the Spooking Sally Challenge. My heart was racing. I'd read everything ever written about dinosaurs — and now I was about to see a real one for the very first time.

The crowd rounded a corner, and came to a sudden halt. The screaming and yelling stopped abruptly, as though somebody had flicked a switch.

And then I saw him.

Bathed in golden spotlights, standing alone on a raised platform in the middle of the room, was a prehistoric monster bigger than anything I had ever seen. He towered over us — rearing up on his hind legs, with his enormous claws extended, ready to strike. Two rows of fearsome white fangs were bared as if in anger; and his great empty eye sockets seemed to bore right through me.

It was the Great Scaly Ockersaurus.

A hush descended on the room as more than a hundred pairs of human eyes stared in wonder. It was like being in church. And then, somebody spoke.

'He's beautiful, isn't he?' said Professor Maxwell Wally quietly, walking into the room. 'Isn't he the most beautiful creature you've ever seen?'

'So tell me, Professor,' demanded Marilyn Miller, shoving a giant furry microphone under the

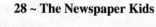

professor's nose. 'Why is this dinosaur so special?'

The cameraman zoomed in on Professor Wally, as he tugged at his little pointy beard and smiled primly.

'Well, Ma'am,' he replied in his American accent, 'until this important discovery in the town of Blue Rock, Australia, experts such as myself had no complete specimen of this particular dinosaur. A few fossils here and there — but nothing this substantial.'

The professor pronounced Australia as though it was AAHHH-stralia. Behind him, about a dozen kids were jumping up and down and waving at the camera, trying to get on television. Porky Merron rolled his eyes back in the sockets until all you could see was white, and stuck his tongue out. Kylie Fletcher had written 'HELLO MUM!' on the back of her Spooking Sally leaflet and was holding it up behind the professor's head.

Spooking Sally . . . I shuddered, and tried not to think about it. I'd managed to avoid Toby and Jasper so far — with any luck, I'd come up with a plausible explanation by the time we met at the Cave this afternoon. If only I could talk to Frankie. I needed her advice badly but she was still busy taking photographs.

'So these old bones must be worth bucketloads of money?' asked Marilyn, glaring at Porky Merron over the professor's shoulder.

'A fortune,' agreed the professor. 'In fact, this skeleton is so rare, one could even say it is priceless — particularly to collectors.'

Mrs Bottomley broke into the interview genteelly. 'That's why the security is so tight,' she told Marilyn. 'The only people allowed to touch the dinosaur are myself and the professor.'

Mrs Bottomley glanced shyly at the professor and patted her rock-solid hairdo. It was one of those curly purple perms that looked a bit like a knitted tea cosy stuck on her head. It went well with her red sniffly nose. 'We're the only ones who know the secret code to switch off the alarm. Ah-Ah-CHOO!' Mrs Bottomley sneezed violently. 'Curses! This wretched hayfever!'

I took a closer look at Neville. He was roped off with white cord to keep the crowds back, but apart from that I couldn't see any other security. Then I spotted the fine red laser beams at the base of the platform. Of course — light sensors! Anyone who broke the beam by stepping across it would set off an alarm. Very clever.

'Excuse me, Professor.' It was Toby's voice. I swung around to see the editor of *Street Wise* nervously pushing his glasses up onto the bridge of his nose. 'The dinosaur seems to have a number of rib bones missing. Is there an explanation for that?'

'Hey! I'm the one doing the interview!' Marilyn turned on him. 'Get lost, kid!'

Toby stared at her stubbornly. 'No offence, Miss Miller, but I don't think you're asking the right questions. According to all the available fossil diagrams, this dinosaur quite clearly has some bones missing . . .'

'What are you talking about? What nonsense!' It was Professor Wally. He looked furious at the interruption. 'The Ockersaurus is perfectly intact. I put him together myself!'

I checked Neville. From this distance he looked all right to me. What was Toby on about?

Mrs Bottomley shook her finger at Toby. 'Toby Trotter! It's not like you to be so rude! The professor is doing an interview for television.' She looked at Professor Wally coyly and batted her eyelids. 'I'm sure he doesn't have time for silly questions.'

'Quite right, Mrs Bottomley.' The professor frowned briefly at Toby, then turned his back on him. His little triangular beard waggled as he smiled at Marilyn Miller. 'Now — where were we?'

'Old Bottoms has got such a crush on the professor,' crowed Jasper. 'Did you see the googly eyes she was making at him? I bet she wants to marry him.'

It was later that day, and the last rays of afternoon sunshine were filtering through the Cave's faded curtains. I was sitting quietly on the couch, patting Scoop and trying to steer Jasper and Toby away from the subject of Sally Champion. I'd been racking my brains ever since we left the museum and I still hadn't thought of how I was going to break the news about the bargain I'd struck with Sally.

'Well, he'd better watch out,' said Toby. 'Mrs Bottomley's already outlived two husbands — he might be the third!'

I sneaked a look at the door. Where on earth was Frankie? She'd know what to do.

'Well, she'll have to get rid of that red nose of hers if she wants the professor to ask her out on a date.' Jasper yawned, losing interest. 'Hey, have we had any replies to the Spooking Sally leaflets?'

My stomach dived into my boots. Any minute now, I'd have to own up.

Toby nodded. 'A couple of kids have come up with ideas already. And I think we'll be swamped with entries after we put it on the Internet.'

'I'm amazed Sally agreed to it,' said Jasper, shaking her head. 'How did you talk her into it, Hugo?'

I gulped, feeling sick. 'Just lucky, I guess.' Stalling for time, I picked up one of the leaflets and read it again.

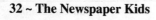

DO YOU LIKE COMPETITIONS?

THEN TRY YOUR HAND AT

THE SPOOKING SALLY CHALLENGE!

Underneath, it explained the rules of the competition. Anyone was allowed to enter by suggesting something they thought would spook Sally. The five best dares would be chosen and Sally had one weekend to attempt them. The first dare to spook Sally would be the winner.

The prize was a basketball personally signed by one of the Blue Rock Bullets, Bobby 'Beanstalk' Buggins. Toby's dad had given it to him for Christmas, forgetting that Toby wasn't exactly the sporting type. Personally, I'd been hoping that the basketball would end up accidentally-on-purpose over at my house. But Toby said he'd been saving it for a special occasion — and this was it.

'Porky Merron wanted us to change it to a girning competition, but I told him it was too late,' said Toby.

'A *what* competition?' Jasper and I stared at him, baffled.

'Girning. It's the proper word for face-pulling. Apparently, they hold the world championships in England each year, and Porky wants to go. He reckons he'd win hands down.'

Jasper grimaced. 'I can't stand Porky Merron. He's got warts.'

'Not any more, he hasn't.' I jumped in, seeing the chance to guide the conversation to safer territory. 'They're gone. His uncle bought them from him.'

'He *bought* Porky's *warts*?' Jasper raised an eyebrow sceptically.

'It's true,' I insisted. 'His uncle paid him twenty cents per wart. All Porky had to do was stop thinking of himself as the owner of the warts. In two weeks, every single one had turned black and dropped off.'

Jasper wrinkled her nose. 'That's disgusting.'

Toby had been listening closely. 'It's also very interesting. If it's true, it could be a medical breakthrough . . .'

I nodded. We all knew that the only proven way to get rid of warts was to cut a potato in half, rub it on the warts, then bury the potato in a patch of ground hit by the light of a full moon. But buying them . . . Toby was right. We could be on to a good story.

I jumped up, relieved to have an excuse to leave. 'I'll get onto it straight away.'

'What's the hurry?' asked Jasper suspiciously. 'Don't you want to talk about the Spooking Sally Challenge?'

'Oh . . . no time like the present,' I replied hastily, backing out the door.

Bang! I'd backed straight into Frankie, who was

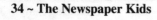

running through the door with a handful of photographs.

'Where've you been?' I hissed. 'I'm in all sorts of trouble . . .'

But Frankie didn't even hear me. She thrust the photos breathlessly at Toby. 'They're still damp . . . I've only just developed them . . . I blew them up as much as I could . . .'

Toby took the photos and flipped through them. I hovered in the doorway, curious to know what he was looking for.

'Hand me the magnifying glass.' Toby peered closely at one of the prints for what seemed like an eternity.

'Well?' said Frankie.

Toby looked up. Behind his thick spectacles, his eyes gleamed triumphantly.

'I was right.' He held a photograph aloft and jabbed at it with his finger. 'Three of Neville's bones are missing, and this photograph proves it!'

Chapter Four

Phew! It looked like I was off the hook for a little bit longer at least.

Toby was so sure he was onto something with the dinosaur bones that there wasn't much point trying to talk to him about anything. He wandered off clutching the photos, muttering feverishly to himself. The last I saw of him that day, he had his nose stuck in the Internet and was busy downloading anything he could about dinosaur anatomy.

That left Jasper, Frankie and me to organise the Spooking Sally Challenge for the weekend. And I couldn't tell her about the deal without Toby being there, could I?

'You're crazy,' said Frankie, shaking her head. 'The longer you leave it, the worse it'll be. Come on — I'll go with you. Let's tell Jasper and get it over and done with.'

'Let's wait a while,' I said hastily. 'No point upsetting Jasper without Toby around to calm her down. There's no telling what she might do.' A vision of my head, stuck on a spike in the front yard, flashed through my mind. It was followed quickly by another vision of my limbs being fed one by one to a tank full of hungry piranhas. Actually, I had quite a good idea of what Jasper might do . . . and none of it was very pleasant.

'Besides,' I added bravely, 'the Challenge starts on Saturday. Chances are we won't even have to tell them. Once Sally sees what we've got lined up for her, she'll be so spooked she'll never show her face around here again.'

'And if she isn't spooked?' asked Frankie.

I took a deep breath. 'Then you'd better organise a ticket to Timbuktu for me. One way.'

The first day of the Spooking Sally Challenge dawned bright and clear. I was over at the Cave by 6.30 am, to pick up any late entries that had come in overnight on E-mail. One of them was from Howard Fitzherbert. 'Get Sally to jump in the shark pool at Marine World just before feeding time,' his entry read. I pressed DELETE, and watched with pleasure as Howard's suggestion scrunched itself up into a ball on screen and floated off to the cyber garbage dump.

Jasper came in a short time later, armed with an official-looking folder and a stopwatch.

'What's that for?' I asked curiously.

'Sally's pulse rate.' Jasper clicked the stopwatch on and off a few times. 'We may have to time it. When people are scared their heart starts pumping. I read about it. Anything over ninety-five beats per minute is a sure sign she's petrified.' She flicked her plaits in a businesslike manner. 'Just in case she tries to pretend she's not.'

I glanced at the list of entries. Just reading them was enough to make my heart race. A lot of them were too dangerous, or just plain stupid like Howard's. But the ones with a tick beside them were the entries that had made it to the 'approved' stage. If it all went according to plan, Sally would be well and truly spooked by one of them by the end of the weekend.

Toby and Frankie arrived fifteen minutes later. Frankie struggled through the door with a tripod, her two best cameras slung around her neck. She wore her dad's old 'on assignment' photographic vest, its pockets bulging with rolls of film and different lenses. Mr Halliday had been a famous photographer, and before he was killed in a car crash, he'd started teaching Frankie everything he knew. That's why she never went anywhere without her cameras. 'The best pictures happen when you least expect them,' she always said. Well, she certainly looked prepared for the unexpected today!

Toby had a mysterious bundle under his arm. When he unfolded it, I saw it was an old white sheet with the words 'Spooking Sally Command Post' painted on it.

'I did it last night,' he said modestly. 'We can hang it up outside the Cave so that everyone knows to come here for information and results.'

'What a great idea, Toby,' said Jasper warmly. 'Here, Hugo and I will help you put it up.' She nudged me. We both knew the banner was Toby's way of making up for the last couple of days. He'd been so preoccupied with his crazy dinosaur theory that Jasper and I had ended up doing all the work for the Spooking Sally Challenge.

To be honest, we both thought the missing bones were a figment of Toby's imagination. He'd been working so hard on *Street Wise* lately, and we knew he was worried about the circulation. Nobody at the museum seemed to think anything was wrong. Jasper and I agreed the bones probably weren't missing at all — Toby just desperately wanted them to be.

We nailed the banner up over the door to the Cave and stood back to admire our handiwork.

'Okay, let's run through the schedule,' said Toby. 'Jasper?'

Jasper snapped to attention. 'Right. Here's what's happening.' She pulled out her folder, turned to a page headed 'RULES!' in big black letters, and cleared her throat.

'The Spooking Sally Challenge starts at 10.00 am sharp. If Sally Champion fails to show up, she automatically loses the Challenge and is publicly exposed as a fibber and a scaredy-cat.'

I thought of Sally's calm hazel eyes staring at Howard as she held the spider. There was no way she wouldn't turn up.

'Toby Trotter will stay behind to man the command post, direct crowds to the next venue, and send the results out over the Internet,' Jasper continued. 'Frankie Halliday will photograph each dare as proof of its success or failure in spooking Sally. Hugo Lilley will be Sally Champion's official minder and will stay as close as possible to her throughout each dare to make sure she completes it.'

That was my idea. If I kept Sally away from Jasper as much as possible, I'd have a better chance of making sure she didn't blab about the reporter's job I'd offered her.

'And I, Jasper Lilley, will be in charge as Chief Organiser and Chief Judge.' Jasper puffed out her chest, looking very pleased with herself. 'That just about wraps it up, I think.'

'Hey! That's not fair!' I said hotly. 'Who decided you were in charge?'

'I did,' replied Jasper grandly. 'Toby's got to stay back here. And you know I'm the best organiser. Look how much I've done already!'

If Toby hadn't stepped in, I probably would have grabbed one of her plaits and choked her with it.

'Break it up, you two,' he ordered. 'Jasper, nobody's saying you shouldn't be the Chief Organiser. You're obviously the best person for the job.'

Jasper smiled smugly.

'. . . but I'm afraid nobody is going to be Chief Judge. We're all in this together. All four of us.'

I grinned as Jasper flounced off, miffed. Good old Toby! He always knew the fairest way to settle an argument. But there was no time to stay angry with each other anyway. The first spectators were starting to gather outside the command post. Any minute now, Sally Champion would arrive — and the Great *Street Wise* Spooking Sally Challenge would begin!

Old Man Crabb was the town miser. He lived in a rickety old wooden house on stilts at the swampy end of town, just near the railway line. Surrounding the house was a two-metre high fence, which was guarded by a savage, stocky pit bull terrier called Bonecrusher.

Mr Crabb was the meanest man in Blue Rock, and he hated everyone except his dog. The rumour was that he had a suitcase full of cash hidden under his bed, but nobody had ever got close enough to see it.

I filled Sally in as we made our way to Mr Crabb's house for the first dare. Sally, as usual, was dressed in her cowgirl outfit and riding her skateboard. Scoop trotted along at my ankles with a stick in his mouth, hoping for a game. Jasper and Frankie followed a short distance behind, discussing the photographs. Bringing up the rear was a mob of about sixteen kids, including Denis Wong who'd come up with the idea.

'Old Man Crabb is so mean he used to make his family wash themselves in the bathrooms at the Blue Rock Shopping Centre to save on hot water,' I told her. 'And when they cleaned their teeth at night, he made them spit into a cup so they could re-use the toothpaste the next day.'

I glanced sideways at Sally to see her reaction. To my disappointment, she didn't look nervous — just interested.

'And they put up with it?' she asked.

I shook my head. 'Nope. One day, about two years ago, Mrs Crabb and all the little Crabbs just packed up and went. It was the rice that did it.'

'The rice?'

'Old Man Crabb used to make them go out on Saturdays — after all the weddings — and pick up the rice off the ground outside churches. Then he'd make Mrs Crabb cook it up in water he'd recycled from Bonecrusher's bath.'

Yep, Charlie Crabb was a skinflint all right. He was such a cheapskate, he even had a little clothesline strung up in the kitchen to dry his tea bags out after he used them. The rumour was he could make one tea bag last a whole month.

But worst of all was the way he used to return his old underpants to Bargain-Mart when the elastic went. Every six months Mr Crabb would take a plastic bag full of his old undies back to the shop and insist they exchange them for new ones. He'd say they were poor quality, that's why they were full of holes. Bargain-Mart had a 'satisfaction guaranteed' policy, so there wasn't much they could do about it. They'd just give Mr Crabb a bagful of new undies and burn the old ones out the back.

The only thing Mr Crabb willingly spent money on was his dog, Bonecrusher. Bonecrusher dined on the best cuts of fillet steak from the local butcher, and his coat was always sleek and shiny, showing off his powerful muscles. Mr Crabb told the vet he didn't mind spending the money, because Bonecrusher kept all the charity collectors away from his house. Bonecrusher, he said, saved him money. He wasn't just a guard dog — he was an investment.

The challenge for Sally Champion was to get past Bonecrusher, knock on Old Man Crabb's front door, and ask the meanest man in Blue Rock for twenty cents.

Denis Wong caught up with us, panting.

'Hey, Sally! You know that pit bulls have special jaws that *lock* when they bite something! They can't let go even if they want to. You have to prise open their mouths with a metal bar!'

Sally stopped her skateboard. 'So?'

'So, aren't you scared that Bonecrusher's gonna grab you by the leg . . . and bite it off?' Denis growled and snapped his teeth a centimetre away from Sally's nose.

Sally laughed. 'I like dogs.' She took the stick out of Scoop's mouth, threw it, then took off again on her skateboard as Scoop raced after it.

Denis grinned at me and made 'cuckoo' circles with his hands. 'Bet she doesn't say that when she opens the gate!' he hissed. Denis was desperate to win the signed basketball. He was so certain his dare

was going to win the Challenge he'd been boasting about it all over town.

Looking at Sally, sailing along on her skateboard with her straight black hair streaming out behind her, I wasn't so sure.

'Remember Sally, you can pull out any time you want.' Jasper held up the stopwatch and clicked the button down with her thumb. 'Your time starts . . . NOW!'

Sally Champion opened the gate and walked into the miser's yard without hesitation.

Nineteen pairs of eyes, glued to cracks in the high wooden fence, watched as Sally sauntered confidently up the dirt pathway. I noticed that she still had the small stick that Scoop had been chasing. I shuddered. If Sally was hoping to frighten Bonecrusher away with that little twig, she had another thing coming.

Suddenly, a loud menacing snarl tore through the silence. I watched in horror as a large, muscular brown dog streaked down the pathway towards Sally Champion with its jaws snapping, its lips pulled back to reveal two rows of razor sharp teeth.

Bonecrusher!

A gasp went up from the fence. 'Don't do it, Sally!' yelled Denis Wong excitedly. 'Run now, while you've still got time!'

'She'll never go through with it!' Jasper whispered.

I heard Frankie shooting frame after frame of film as Bonecrusher launched himself through the air towards Sally. Scoop whimpered, smelling our fear. My heart was thumping. Why didn't Sally run?

But Sally just stood there, as still as a statue. She had her back to us, but I could tell by the way she was standing that she wasn't the slightest bit afraid. She wasn't cowering, or even trembling. In fact, she seemed to be staring straight into Bonecrusher's eyes as he launched himself towards her throat . . .

Then, something very strange happened. Mid-air, Bonecrusher seemed to change his mind. He dropped to the ground and stood there, still snarling.

Very, very slowly, Sally Champion lowered herself onto her haunches until her eyes were only centimetres from the pit bull's. He lunged at her and snapped his teeth, but she didn't flinch.

Sally crouched there motionless, while Bonecrusher sniffed her face, and then her hands. He was still growling, but it was a long way back in his throat.

Behind the fence, nobody dared to breathe. The only sound was the clicking of Frankie's camera shutter as Sally s-l-o-w-l-y raised her hand and showed Bonecrusher the small stick.

The dog's eyes locked onto the stick. Slowly and deliberately, Sally drew a circle in the dirt. Bonecrusher watched intently. He'd stopped growling.

Sally drew a straight line in front of the circle, and gently laid the stick in the dirt. Then she stood up, and continued walking up the path towards the door.

I couldn't believe my eyes. Bonecrusher wasn't moving. He just stood there with a dopey look on his face, staring at the line Sally had drawn in the dirt with the stick.

'She's . . . she's *hypnotised* him!' whispered Jasper in awe. 'She hypnotised Bonecrusher!'

I blinked a couple of times to make sure I wasn't seeing things. I knew you could hypnotise chooks that way . . . but guard dogs?

The next thing I knew, Sally was skipping back down the path waving something shiny in the air.

'He gave me a dollar!' Sally's face was shining with glee. 'I said I only wanted twenty cents but he made me take a dollar. Does that count?'

For once, my bossy big sister was almost lost for words. 'The old cheapskate gave you a dollar?' asked Jasper faintly. 'A *dollar*?'

Sally nodded. 'Mr Crabb said I deserved it for showing him the weakness in his security system. He's going to get another guard dog now to keep Bonecrusher's mind on the job. I told him it's a lot harder to hypnotise two dogs at once.'

She flicked the gold coin with her thumb and

watched it tumble through the air, glinting in the sunlight, before she caught it again.

'So? Did I pass the first dare?'

Jasper frowned. She still looked like she couldn't believe it. 'It looks like it,' she said ungraciously. She placed a large tick in her folder. 'I guess I should say . . . congratulations.'

'Thanks.' Sally grinned wickedly. 'Well, what are we waiting for? NEXT!'

Chapter Five

'I can't watch.' Frankie pulled her baseball cap down over her eyes and handed me her camera. 'Here. It's focused. You take the picture, Hugo. Just tell me when she's back on the ground.'

I peered through the camera, and tilted it up until I found Sally. She was a tiny speck about three-quarters of the way up the ladder. Another fifteen metres, and she'd be on the platform of Jungle Jim's Bungee Jump. Dare number two.

'Are you all right, Frankie?' I heard her breathing in short, shallow gasps, and put down the camera.

'I'm . . . okay,' she said. 'It's just . . . heights. I can't even watch somebody up that high or I go all funny.'

Watching Sally attempt her second dare, I was feeling a bit queasy myself. Jungle Jim's Bungee Jump was a rusty old rig which hadn't been used for years. Back when bungee jumping was all the rage, Jungle Jim did a roaring trade. Dozens of people lined up every day, happy to pay a hundred dollars each for the privilege of being scared witless. Day after day, they climbed the ladder, tied the long thick rubber bands around their ankles and dived off the platform to the cry of '3 — 2 — 1 BUNGEEEE!'. It looked like they were going to land right on their head and be splattered all over the ground — but the rubber bungee cord always stopped them just before they did. Jasper and I used to sit on the grass and watch them, bouncing up and down and yelling their heads off.

But it didn't last. There was a rumour somebody's eyes had popped right out of their head from the pressure of the rubber band, and after that, people went off the idea. Nobody had climbed up the rickety old ladder onto Jungle Jim's Bungee Jump platform for two years. Nobody, that is — until now.

'She's done it!' A cheer went up from the crowd, which had grown to about thirty-five kids. I took a picture of Sally waving from the platform. She was at least six storeys off the ground. For the hundredth time, I thanked my lucky stars I'd had to stay back and look after Frankie. Otherwise, as Sally's minder, I would have been up there with her. My stomach flopped around like a stranded fish just thinking about it.

'Okay, Sally, you can come back down!' yelled Jasper, putting another tick in her folder.

I pretended to fiddle with the camera, trying to hide my disappointment. So Sally Champion wasn't scared of heights either. I'd been hoping she would chicken out before she got to the top of the platform. That would have solved my problem in an instant.

'Sally!' Jasper stood at the foot of the ladder with her hands on her hips. 'I said you can come down!'

There was no movement from the platform. 'What on earth is she doing?' I heard Jasper mutter.

My heart leapt. Maybe it was delayed shock. Maybe Sally was so frightened she couldn't move . . .

'Oh, crikey, she's going to jump!'

Frankie blurted out the words just as I saw Sally open the safety barrier and shuffle calmly to the edge of the platform.

A nervous murmur swept through the crowd.

'Sally . . . Sally, get back . . .' I called helplessly. But the wind carried away my words. Instead, floating down from the platform came an unmistakable cry.

'3 — 2 — 1 . . . BUNGEEE!!!!'

It was a perfect swan dive. The fringes of Sally's cowgirl outfit floated gracefully behind her as she plummeted towards the ground.

'AAAGGHHHH!' Somebody screamed — but it wasn't Sally. I looked around for Frankie and saw her being sick behind the bushes.

The only sound coming from Sally was a deep, gurgling laugh — and the loud BOING-ing noise as the rubber band snapped her away from the ground and bounced her almost as high as the platform again. She flapped her arms like bird's wings and laughed with delight as she glided through the air. After bouncing a few more times, she gradually came to rest, hanging upside down by the ankles.

'You nearly scared us all to death,' scolded Jasper, as we untied Sally and helped her stand up. 'Here, give me your wrist. I'm going to take your pulse rate. I don't care what you say, Sally Champion, you must have been terrified.'

The crowd fell silent as Jasper searched Sally's wrist for a pulse, then started the stopwatch. The sixty seconds ticked by so slowly they felt like sixty years. I crossed my fingers and waited impatiently. Jasper was right — she had to be scared. Even a professional stuntman couldn't do what Sally had just done without their heart-rate going up.

Jasper looked up. A mixture of disbelief and confusion flitted across her face.

'There must be some mistake . . .' She shook the stopwatch and held it to her ear.

'Why? What is it?' I had a feeling I'd be better off not knowing — but I couldn't help myself. 'What's her heart-rate?'

'Forty-five,' replied Jasper quietly. 'Forty-five beats per minute.' She looked at me wide-eyed. 'That's slower than a normal person's resting heart-rate.'

That's when I knew I was really in trouble.

Howard Fitzherbert was sprawled on the footpath outside the milk bar, burning ants with a magnifying glass.

'Hey, Metal Mouth!' he yelled rudely at Sally. 'Wanna help me barbecue some ants?'

Sally's spurs tinkled as she jumped off her skateboard, and stood looking down at Howard.

'No thanks, Howard. I've come to have a chat with you. And my name's not Metal Mouth.'

Jasper clicked the stopwatch. 'Your time starts . . . now,' she whispered under her breath.

Howard looked up and saw the crowd. By now, there were about sixty of us. Word was spreading fast that there was nothing — *nothing* — that Sally Champion wouldn't do. And that included taking on the school bully. Dare number three.

'Too gutless to come here alone, hey, Smelly Champion?' said Howard lazily, a cruel smile spreading over his face.

'Not at all. They're just here to watch the fun.' Sally reached down and whipped the magnifying glass out of Howard's hand before he knew what was happening. 'Now, why don't you stop torturing poor defenceless insects for two seconds and listen to me?'

Howard jumped up, his eyes narrow slits of rage. He was the biggest kid at Blue Rock Primary, and next to Sally he looked like a giant.

'Maybe I should torture *you* for a while, spider girl,' he hissed. Howard lunged at Sally and grabbed the hand that was holding the magnifying glass. Wrenching it out of her hand, he twisted her arm behind her back and held the magnifying glass up to the sun. Then slowly, with a nasty leer on his face, he started to direct the burning rays onto Sally's arm.

'You're Chinese, aren't you?' taunted Howard. 'Then how about a Chinese burn?'

'NO!' I ran forward and tried to head-butt Howard's back. He swatted me away like a fly.

'Stay out of it, Hugo.' It was Sally's voice, as calm and cheerful as always. Surprised, I noticed she had somehow managed to slip out of Howard's grip. Howard looked surprised too. 'Hey! How did you . . .'

'Now, listen here, you big bully.' Sally's spurs jangled as she danced tantalisingly just out of Howard's reach. He made another clumsy run at her, and she sidestepped neatly out of his way. 'First of all, I'm Vietnamese-Australian — so get it right. Second — from now on, you're going to stop picking on people. You're just a big clumsy oaf with a personality problem and it's time you grew up.'

Howard stood there breathing heavily, clenching and unclenching his fists. 'Nobody tells me what to do . . . nobody . . .'

Sally stopped dancing and regarded him seriously. 'That's a very sad attitude you've got, Howard. Perhaps if you changed it, you might make some friends and . . .'

She didn't get to finish her sentence. Bellowing with rage, Howard Fitzherbert launched himself at Sally Champion like a cannonball, his arms flailing in all directions.

It was all over in the blink of an eye.

All I remember is Sally standing quite still, with that strange, calm smile on her face and Howard Fitzherbert hurtling towards her. Just as he reached her, she made a quick movement with her arms and stepped backwards.

The next thing I knew, Howard was lying flat on his back, gasping for air.

'Help . . . can't breathe . . .' I heard him wheeze.

Sally bent over him and gave him a friendly pat.

'You'll be fine in a minute. You just knocked the wind out of yourself when you fell.'

A fat tear rolled down Howard's face. 'You . . . you *hit* me!'

Sally shook her head. 'No, Howard, I didn't hit you.'

Sixty curious faces stared down at Howard Fitzherbert, the school bully, lying flat on his back blubbering like a baby.

'Then how . . . ?' I ventured.

'It's called aikido,' replied Sally. 'You harness the power of your attacker, and use it against them.' She prodded Howard gently with the toe of her cowboy boot. 'You see, Howard, violence never solves anything. I never touched you. You did this to yourself.'

Jasper checked the stopwatch. 'Two minutes and thirty-seven seconds. Not bad, Sally.'

As we walked on to the next dare, there was a new spring in every kid's step.

I looked back and saw Howard Fitzherbert sitting up staring after us, rubbing his head. There was a look in his eyes I'd never seen before.

Respect.

'The headless body lay face down in a shallow grave,' intoned Jasper in a deep, macabre voice. The candle flickered, casting an eerie yellow light on her freckled face.

'How could it be lying face down if it didn't have

a head?' interrupted Sally Champion, sitting up in her sleeping bag.

Jasper frowned. 'Well, it just *did* . . . Oh, you've gone and ruined it now!'

'I'm scared!' wailed Kylie Fletcher.

'I'm not,' said Sally. 'Pass the snakes, somebody.'

I wriggled out of my sleeping bag and felt around in the dark for the lollies. The Spooky Slumber Party wasn't exactly going to plan. By now, Sally was supposed to be so scared by Jasper's ghost stories that there would be no way she'd go to the graveyard, alone, at midnight — the witching hour. That was the fourth dare, and the scariest so far. It was so scary that none of us were brave enough to go with her. So to prove she'd done it, Sally had to bring back a small amethyst crystal I had placed on one of the graves earlier that day.

And the way things were going, she might just do it.

I turned to Toby, trying to control my panic. 'What if Sally completes this dare as well?' I whispered.

Toby looked at me oddly, his large spectacles glinting in the candlelight. 'You know the deal — if Sally wins the Challenge, she wins the basketball. If she doesn't, somebody else wins it. What are you so worried about?'

'Nothing.' I tried to ignore the sick, cold feeling in my stomach.

'What's that noise?' shrieked Ella Mahmoud. A whining, scratching sound filled the room. It was coming from the window.

Everyone's eyes swivelled nervously towards the window. Everyone burrowed deeper into the safety of their sleeping bags. Everyone, that is, except Sally Champion. She was too busy digging through the bag of lollies looking for a snake.

'It's the head,' whispered Jasper dramatically. 'The head off the headless body . . . it wanders the earth, unable to rest . . .'

'Come on in, Head!' yelled Sally Champion. 'Come and join the party!'

Kylie and Ella started crying.

'Oh, stop being so silly!' said Sally, rolling her eyes. She ran to the window and pulled back the curtain. 'Look! It's only a tree branch, rubbing on the glass.'

Jasper suddenly lost her temper. 'Sit down, Sally! You're spoiling it for everyone.'

Sally yawned, and looked at her watch. 'Look, if it's all right with everyone, I might go to the graveyard. It's nearly midnight.'

'Fine,' snapped Jasper. 'I hope you get chased by a werewolf.'

'. . . Jeremiah Budd, born 1897, died 1978. He's buried on the western side of the graveyard, just next to the

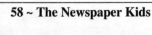

Fitzherbert family crypt. It's the one covered with wild jasmine. That's where you'll find the amethyst.'

I held the candle up to Sally's face, feeling a pang of guilt that I was sending her out alone. 'Are you sure you'll be all right? You can always back out, you know,' I added hopefully.

Sally laughed softly. 'And lose the Challenge? Not on your life!' She opened the back door, and took a deep breath of cool fresh air. 'I'm going to win this, Hugo Lilley — and I'm not going to let a few old ghosts and werewolves stop me!'

With a heavy heart, I watched as she slipped into the darkness and disappeared.

The minutes ticked by. My mind was in turmoil. What if Sally completed the Challenge and returned from the graveyard with the amethyst? Worse still — what if she didn't? Either way I was in deep trouble.

'Maybe she's chickened out and gone home,' yawned Jasper. 'Either that, or a vampire's grabbed her.'

'Don't joke about it,' I said gloomily.

My glow-in-the-dark watch was showing 12.29 when I heard the back door open. Ten seconds later, Sally slipped into the lounge room, her bare feet wet with dew and speckled with grass seeds.

In one hand, she held a bunch of freshly picked wild jasmine. In the other, she held the amethyst.

The purple crystal glowed softly as Sally held it up triumphantly to the candlelight.

'Hmmph!' sniffed Jasper. 'Looks like you've done it again, Sally. I'm starting to believe you really *aren't* scared of anything!'

Sally jumped into her sleeping bag and zipped it up. 'Oh, it's easy to be brave when you consider the prize,' she said casually.

My blood froze in my veins.

'You're doing all of this for a basketball?' asked Toby, sitting up and rubbing his eyes wearily.

Sally looked at him, puzzled.

'Not the basketball, Toby. The job on *Street Wise*.'

The only sound was the branch of the old ironbark rubbing on the window — and my heart, thudding against my chest like a cannon.

'A job on *Street Wise*?' repeated Toby slowly.

'A job ... on *Street Wise*?' snapped Jasper, suddenly wide awake.

Sally snuggled into her sleeping bag and closed her eyes.

'The reporter's job,' she said sleepily. 'You know. The one that Hugo offered me.'

Chapter Six

'**Y**ou ... IDIOT!' yelled Jasper. She slammed the Cave door shut with a bang.

I stared back at her miserably, lost for words. It was ten o'clock the next morning, and everyone from the slumber party had gone home. Toby sat slumped on one of the old couches, his head buried in his hands. For once, he didn't say a word in my defence.

'Why did you tell Sally she could work on *Street Wise*? Why didn't you tell us?' Jasper's eyes were blazing. She grabbed my shirt sleeve and shook me like a rag doll. 'Why?'

The only sound was the rain pelting down on the Cave's tin roof. I felt hot tears pricking the back of my eyes as I searched desperately for an answer. This was the worst fight we'd ever had, and I felt like there was nothing I could do to stop it.

Frankie spoke up. 'Don't be so mean, Jasper. Hugo thought he was doing the right thing. Maybe he made a mistake, that's all. We all make mistakes.'

'Some mistake!' fumed Jasper. She let go my sleeve and pushed me away in disgust. 'You obviously forgot to take your intelligence pills that day, Hugo.'

I tried to reason with her. 'What's so bad about having Sally on *Street Wise* anyway? She's fun.'

'I like her, too,' agreed Frankie stoutly. 'Look at all the brave things she did yesterday.'

'That's not the point!' shouted Jasper. '*Street Wise* is like a club. A special club. You can't just let *anyone* in.'

'You let *me* in,' Frankie pointed out. 'You didn't want me in *Street Wise*, remember, Jasper? And look how well it's all turned out.'

'That was different.' Jasper blushed. 'You're a photographer. And you're Hugo's best friend. We don't even *know* Sally Champion.'

She glowered at me. 'And now, thanks to Blabber Mouth, she's part of our newspaper.'

'Only if she wins the Challenge,' I snapped, fed up with Jasper's tirade. 'That was the deal, remember? If we can find something to scare her . . .'

'Oh, sure,' Jasper sneered. 'She's not scared of spiders. Or savage dogs. Or heights. Or Howard Fitzherbert. Or ghosts. Or the dark.' She turned on me in fury. 'Face it, Hugo — Sally's going to win the Challenge and it's *all your fault*!'

'Fine!' I yelled, heading for the door. Scoop scampered after me. 'Go right ahead and blame me! And you know what? I don't care any more Jasper because . . . because . . . I QUIT!'

The words popped out of my mouth before I could stop them.

'If Hugo goes, so do I,' said Frankie loyally, stomping after me. 'I quit, too.' She bent down and patted Scoop. 'And so does he.'

Yikes! I thought. Too late to back out now.

'Oh, great!' wailed Jasper. A big sob tumbled unexpectedly out of her mouth. 'No chief reporter. No photographer. No guard dog. Just a silly girl on a skateboard who's never written a story in her life.'

She dived into the vacant couch headfirst and started howling into the cushions. 'We may as well close *Street Wise*. It's all *ruined*!'

'Come on, Hugo.' Frankie opened the door. 'Let's go to my place.'

I hesitated, staring out into the rain. The four of us had started *Street Wise*. We'd had so many adventures together; so many meetings in the Cave.

And now it was ending like this — with a terrible fight, and everybody hating each other.

'Come back inside.' For the first time that day, Toby spoke. He lifted his head from his hands and looked at us wearily. 'Nobody is going anywhere, and nobody is quitting. Sit down.'

We sat.

Toby sighed deeply. 'Now, listen to me, all of you.' He stood up and started pacing the room.

'There's no denying we're in a difficult position. Hugo — as chief reporter of *Street Wise* — has made a verbal contract with Sally that we are legally and morally obliged to honour.'

'What does that mean?' I whispered to Frankie.

'It means you shook hands on a deal, and we have to stick to it,' Frankie whispered back.

Toby frowned briefly at us.

'This is not a perfect situation, but it's not the disaster everybody seems to think it is. And it's certainly not bad enough to destroy our friendship *and* the newspaper.'

I started to cheer up. Maybe there was a solution after all.

'Here's my suggestion,' continued Toby. 'The Challenge isn't over yet. We have one more shot at spooking Sally. And at the same time, we'll see if she's got what it takes to be a reporter on *Street Wise*.'

He blinked at us through his thick glasses. 'We'll give Sally the chance to prove herself by assigning her the toughest and scariest job on the newspaper.'

Jasper sat up, sniffing back her tears. 'What's that?'

'Yeah, what do you mean?' Frankie and I were puzzled, too.

Toby looked at us in surprise.

'The dinosaur bones, of course. Our front page story. Final dare.'

That's how the six of us — Toby, Jasper, Frankie, Sally, Scoop and me — came to be huddled underneath the old fig tree outside the Blue Rock Museum that night. It was ten o'clock, and pouring with rain.

I wiped my dripping face and thought longingly of my cosy bed. If it wasn't for the fight, and the Spooking Sally Challenge, and Toby's crazy dinosaur theory, that's where I'd be. But this was our last chance to win the Challenge. Not only that — once Sally saw how hard it was being a reporter, maybe she'd lose interest. Then things could go back to the way they used to be.

'How are we going to get in?' whispered Frankie, breaking the silence. 'Look. There's a guard on the door.'

Peering through the darkness into the dimly lit

lobby of the museum, I could see a bored security guard lolling in a chair with his cap tipped forward over his eyes, puffing on a cigarette.

'He's been there ever since Neville went on show,' Jasper replied. 'To make sure nobody steals anything.'

An awkward silence fell. I knew Jasper was thinking the same thing as I was. *Nobody's stolen any dinosaur bones. How could they? Not with the guard there. Toby's made a mistake. He's just imagining things . . .*

'I know you think I'm crazy,' said Toby stubbornly, reading my mind. 'But I'm sure something's going on. Frankie's photographs prove it. There are three rib bones missing, and it's up to us to find out what's happened to them.'

'Well, *I* don't think you're crazy,' said Sally. 'I think you're right. And imagine catching a dinosaur thief in the act!' I could see her pink and green braces glowing in the dark as she grinned excitedly. 'Come on . . . let's climb this tree. We can get in through one of the skylights on the roof of the museum.'

She clambered up onto the lowest branch and looked down at us. 'Well? What are you waiting for?'

The rest of us looked at each other nervously. Even Toby didn't look as keen any more.

'It looks pretty dark up there,' he gulped, shining his miniature Swiss Army torch up the tree. 'Maybe we'd better forget about it . . .'

Of course! Toby was scared of the dark. Maybe I'd be back in bed sooner than I thought.

'Don't think about it, Toby,' said Sally cheerfully. 'Keep your mind off it by concentrating on this tongue twister: red leather, yellow leather.'

'Red leather, yellow leather,' repeated Toby doubtfully, putting the torch back in his pocket.

'Good. Say that as quickly as you can, over and over, and you'll soon forget about the dark.' Sally bent down and hauled Toby up onto the branch with her before he could argue.

Jasper looked at Sally resentfully and shrugged. 'Well, if Toby can do it, so can I.'

I watched as she disappeared up the tree after the others. I could hear Toby mumbling 'Rella yedda . . . no . . . red lella . . . oops . . .'

'Hey! What about spiders!' I whispered fiercely, clambering after them. I didn't mind climbing wet, slippery trees in the day when I could see properly, but what if I put my hand on a big hairy spider in the dark?

Sally's voice floated down, reassuring me. 'Spiders hate the wet. They'll all be in their holes, keeping warm and dry.'

The museum was a big square building that was supposed to be a great example of modern architecture. To me it looked like a giant concrete shoe box with windows in it. Just like a shoe box, it had a perfectly flat top. And as luck would have it, one of the old fig's giant branches hung right over it.

It was only when we were all up there, standing on the roof, that I realised Frankie wasn't with us.

I looked down. She was huddled against the tree trunk with her cameras slung around her neck and Scoop at her feet.

'I — can't — do — it.' Her terrified whisper barely reached us.

'We'll have to go back,' I told Sally firmly. 'She's scared of heights. And we can't do this without a photographer.'

But before I had time to move, Sally had scooted past me. I watched as she scrambled down the tree and jumped onto the ground beside Frankie. I heard whispering, then Frankie's voice raised in panic: 'No! No! No!'

'What's she up to?' Jasper said irritably. 'Let's go back. I'm getting soaked.'

'Wait.' I could hear the two girls talking again. Sally's voice, low and calm, seemed to be reassuring Frankie. Then I saw Frankie do something she'd never done before — she took her two precious cameras from around her neck and handed them to Sally.

Sally hung the cameras around her own neck. I heard her murmur something else to Frankie. Then, as I watched in disbelief, Sally began to climb the tree again — and Frankie followed her.

'Hang on to my fringes,' I heard Sally say. 'I'll guide you up. Don't look down, and don't forget the magic words.'

Magic words?

I heard Frankie mumbling something as she climbed higher. It sounded like 'Nyik . . . nyook . . . Oh, bother . . . oo-nik nyak . . .'

I held my breath. Frankie looked terrified, but she didn't stop. She just hung on grimly to Sally's cowboy pants and repeated the strange words over and over, like a spell.

When the two of them finally made it onto the roof, Frankie was shaking like a leaf. But her eyes were shining as she grabbed my arm.

'I did it, Hugo!' she crowed triumphantly. 'I beat it! I faced my fear, and now it'll never scare me that much *ever again*!'

'Same here,' I heard Toby murmur proudly.

I turned to Sally, mystified. 'How did you talk her into it?'

Sally shrugged modestly. 'Oh, it's the magic words. They never fail. Unique New York.'

'Unique New York?'

Sally grinned as she handed the cameras back to Frankie. 'The world's hardest tongue twister. Try and say it quickly four times without fudging it. Guaranteed to make you forget everything else. Even fear.'

The five of us stared down at the skylight. It was a clear square of thick plastic, designed to let light into one of the museum's dark inner rooms. The roof was dotted with them.

'Isn't this breaking and entering?' I asked nervously. 'Won't we get into trouble with the police?'

'It's only break and enter if you break something, dummy,' said Jasper.

She shot a sly look at Sally. 'Of course, we'll still get into terrible trouble if we're caught. Our parents will kill us.'

I knew immediately what Jasper was up to. Our parents were a pair of old softies. They did a lot of yelling, but we only pretended to be scared of them so they didn't feel like failures. But maybe Sally's were different. Maybe the one thing she was scared of was making her parents angry . . .

'Not a chance,' said Sally dismissively. 'We just won't get caught. Simple as that.' She struggled with the rusty catch on the skylight, then eased it open. I strained my eyes and made out the shape of a row of sinks below.

'It's the bathroom.'

'Here, I'll go first,' declared Toby bravely, climbing into the opening. Grabbing onto the edge of the skylight, he slowly lowered himself into the darkness below. He looked up at us and grinned. 'If you hear a splash, you'll know I've fallen in the toilet.' Then he let go.

I heard a thud and a grunt, as Toby landed on the floor below.

Jasper, Sally and Frankie followed him through the skylight, then it was my turn. I took a last look at Blue Rock from the museum roof, enjoying the light drizzle and brisk breeze on my face. I started to hum a little tune as I sat down and swung my legs into the skylight hole.

Maybe I got too cocky. Or maybe I just lost my concentration for a minute.

All I know is that as I started to lower myself down, something brushed against my face. Something light and tickly. Something that felt like . . .

A spider?

'AAGGHH!' With a terrified yell, I let go and plummeted through the hole, swiping desperately at my face with my hands. I hit the hard tiled floor with a thump, landing heavily on my arm.

A split second later, there was a sickening snap.

Chapter Seven

'**Q**uick. Somebody's coming.'

Toby helped me onto my feet. I moaned softly as a sharp pain shot up my arm.

'The guard must have heard the noise,' he said.

We shrank back against the cold tiled walls, hearing the sound of footsteps running up the hallway outside.

'Professor, was that you?' a man's voice called.

The door of the bathroom opened. The bright beam of a flashlight flickered briefly around the room. It passed so close to us I could almost feel it. Squeezed into the far corner, none of us breathed. I clenched my teeth to stop myself from groaning, and prayed that he wouldn't swing the flashlight up to the ceiling and see the open skylight. The pain was getting worse. My whole arm felt like it was on fire.

'Hmm ... that's funny,' the man's voice said. 'Could have sworn I heard something ...'

'It was probably the storm, Angelo.' This time I recognised the voice. It was American. Professor Maxwell Wally must have been working late at the museum. 'Don't worry about it. I'd say the wind has blown a branch onto the ...'

The voices faded as the footsteps disappeared out of earshot.

'Phew,' breathed Toby. He switched on his torch and shone it on my face. 'That was close. Are you all right, Hugo?'

I winced. 'I think my arm's broken. There was a spider on my face, I couldn't help it ...'

'It wasn't a spider, it was a leaf.' Sally brushed it out of my hair and showed it to me. 'See? The wind must have blown it.'

Toby shone his torch on my arm. I heard the others gasp and looked down. Between the elbow and the wrist, where there should have been a straight line, the bone stuck out at right angles, making a strange sort of tent under the skin.

'Oh, gross,' groaned Jasper, covering her eyes. 'We'll have to call the security guard. I think I'm going to faint ...'

'Stay calm!' Toby said. 'We can't let anybody know we're here.' He looked at us grimly. 'We'll have to call off the dinosaur investigation. There's no way we can stay here all night. We have to get Hugo home as soon as possible. We can think up a story to explain his arm once we're out of here.'

I closed my eyes and tried to ignore the pain. How on earth was I going to sneak past the guard, let alone make it home through the rain and wind, and then climb in my bedroom window? Every small jolt sent shockwaves of agony through my body.

'He can't walk home like this,' said Frankie urgently, reading my mind. 'You have to keep his arm still. We'll have to do something with it.'

'Does anyone know first aid?' asked Sally.

There was silence.

'Don't look at me!' squeaked Jasper. 'I fainted at the sight of blood at that first aid course, remember? Imagine what touching *that* would do to me! Uggh!'

'You have to do it,' ordered Toby. 'We need to put Hugo's arm in a sling to keep it still. You're the only one who knows how.'

Jasper backed into the corner shaking her head. 'No way. I'm terrified of that sort of stuff . . .'

'So? I'm scared of heights and I still climbed the tree,' said Frankie angrily.

Toby nodded. 'And I'm scared of the dark . . . or at least, I was,' he corrected himself.

Jasper covered her face with her hands and whimpered. 'Stop it! Stop it! I can't do it! I can't even look at it . . .'

I cradled my arm gingerly and said nothing. We were in a terrible fix and I had no idea how we were going to get out of it. The missing dinosaur bones and the Spooking Sally Challenge had vanished from my mind completely. All I could think about was my aching arm, and how we were going to get out of the museum without getting caught.

Sally sighed in exasperation. 'Well, if you won't do it Jasper, then I will. But you'll have to tell me how.'

Jasper peeked at Sally between her fingers. Even in the dark I could tell she was annoyed. '*You'll* do it? You don't know the first thing about first aid.' She put her hands on her hips. 'I'm the only one who's qualified, Sally Champion. I've got a *certificate*.'

'Of course, you're the expert,' replied Sally respectfully. 'So perhaps you can supervise me. Tell me how to make a sling and I'll fix Hugo's arm myself.'

Jasper was silent.

'Please, Sis,' I said weakly.

'Hugo's hurt. We need your help, Jasper,' said Toby quietly. 'We can't do this without you.'

Jasper sneaked another look at my arm and shuddered. I saw her glance defiantly at Sally. Then, she straightened her shoulders and took a deep breath.

'Right-o. If I'm going to make a sling, I need some material,' she declared, suddenly swinging into action. 'Toby, cut me off a length of that roller-towel with your penknife. And make sure it's a long piece . . . long enough to tie a knot in . . .'

As I listened to Jasper issuing orders like a bossy Florence Nightingale, Sally Champion caught my eye — and winked.

'Okay, here's the plan.' Toby licked his finger and squeakily drew a map on the bathroom mirror with it. 'Here's where we are. There's the closest fire exit. If we cut through the dinosaur display, we should be able to escape without anybody seeing us. That way we can also take a quick look at Neville to see if those rib bones are still missing.'

'What about Professor Wally?' I could see my reflection by torch-light in the mirror. The roller-towel sling around my neck looked pretty silly, but it was doing the job, and already I was feeling a little better.

Toby frowned. 'Hopefully, he's gone home by now. Otherwise he'll be in his office working. We'll just have to be very quiet.'

Silently, we crept out of the bathroom and down the darkened hallway. I thought of Scoop, waiting outside for us, and hoped that he hadn't wandered off. The rain was still pelting down. With any luck, the dull pounding on the roof and the eerie howling of the wind would mask any small sounds we might make.

As we tiptoed towards the dinosaur room, I couldn't help feeling excited — and a little bit scared. Being in the same room as a two hundred million year old dinosaur was one thing when there were heaps of other people there too; being there on our own in the middle of the night was quite another.

'What if the old bones come alive at midnight and the dinosaurs take over the museum?' I whispered, half-wanting to believe it. 'Can you imagine the ghost of the Ockersaurus stalking us, like prey?'

Frankie shivered. 'Shut up, you're giving me the creeps.'

Sally turned around and grinned at me, her pink and green braces glowing in the dark. 'Look, there's Neville prowling the corridors,' she said, pointing behind me. 'Do-you-think-he-saurus?'

Despite my throbbing arm, I giggled.

'Ssshhh!' Toby put his finger to his lips. We were almost at the large open area where Neville was displayed. Judging by the fingers of light reaching into the dark corridor, the rare dinosaur was illuminated even at night. Without the cover of darkness to hide us, we would have to be careful.

Toby gestured at us to stay flat against the wall while he checked that the coast was clear. Then, peering cautiously around the corner, he beckoned us to follow.

'The display cabinets next to Neville,' he hissed. 'Everyone make a run for them — and keep your head down.'

I held my sling to keep my arm still, and sprinted across the floor after the others. We crouched down behind the display cabinets, catching our breath before the final dash to the fire exit. Peering over the cabinet, I could see the red 'EMERGENCY EXIT' sign glowing at the other side of the room.

Toby gave us the thumbs up. So far, so good. There was no sign of Professor Wally or the security guard. 'Look at Neville!' he whispered, pointing up.

I looked, and once again was struck dumb with awe. Even though I had seen the Ockersaurus just a few days before, somehow, at night, he looked different. Bigger, more majestic even than the pictures I had seen of the T-rex. I gazed at his giant frame looming over us, and imagined Neville roaming the grassy plains of Blue Rock in search of dinner all those millions of years ago. He could have scoffed a whole tribe of cave people in one sitting if he'd wanted to.

'The rib cage!' whispered Toby impatiently. 'The bones are definitely missing. There should be sixteen on each side . . . see?'

As I started counting, Toby craned his neck over the cabinet and nearly fell over.

'Look . . . look . . . foot . . .' he spluttered, gesturing wildly.

'Speak English, Toby,' whispered Jasper.

'Shouldn't we get going?' asked Frankie anxiously.

Toby turned to us excitedly. 'It's not just the three ribs — now the largest bone from the right foot is missing. I can tell even without my diagrams!'

I took a quick peek over the cabinet. It looked like Toby was right. The left foot had two long bones that connected Neville's toes and his ankle joint. On the right foot, there was a space where one of those bones should have been. All you could see were the bits of wire that were supposed to go through the middle of the bone to connect it to the rest of the skeleton.

Something else was bothering me — the red laser beams I had seen around the base of the dinosaur were no longer there. That meant the alarm was switched off. Maybe Toby's idea wasn't so crazy after all. Somebody was definitely tampering with the dinosaur.

'Cool!' breathed Sally. 'Somebody is stealing the dinosaur, bit by bit!'

'I'll take a photo,' whispered Frankie. 'More evidence, in case we need it.'

Just then, I heard a sound that made my blood run cold. Footsteps. Slow, deliberate footsteps — and they were heading our way.

I felt the others freeze. They'd heard the footsteps, too. Toby lifted his finger to his lips but didn't make a sound. I could feel my heart thudding in my chest, and wondered if the others were as scared as I was.

Crouched behind the display case, desperately trying to protect my arm, I lifted my eyes and saw a large black shadow on the wall behind the Ockersaurus. I couldn't see the person that the footsteps belonged to, but judging by the shadow it was a giant of a man — nearly half as tall as the Ockersaurus — it was much too big to be the security guard or Professor Wally. It looked like the newspaper kids weren't the only intruders in the museum.

I forced myself to look at the shadow again. It was getting closer. Whoever it was had some sort of long object in their hand. A gun? I broke out in a cold sweat. This was the rarest and most valuable dinosaur skeleton in the world. 'Absolutely priceless,' the professor had told Marilyn Miller.

'Especially to collectors.' How far would a mad collector go to get their hands on it? And what would they do if they saw us?

The footsteps reached the dinosaur and stopped. I hunched into a tight ball and buried my face in my lap. As much as I hated to admit it, I was scared stiff. Too scared to be a crime reporter and take notes. Too scared to even watch what was happening. On one side, I could feel Frankie shaking like a leaf. On the other side, Jasper's teeth were chattering. I couldn't see Toby but I was sure he would be just as petrified as we were.

And Sally? A sudden thought struck me. *Maybe Sally was scared, too.* And if she was, we had won the Challenge!

The only problem was, I had to see for myself. If Sally had finally been spooked, then we needed a witness to prove it.

I opened my eyes just in time to see Sally leap out from behind the cabinet with a shout that echoed throughout the museum.

'STOP THIEF! My name is Sally Champion and I am making a citizen's arrest on behalf of . . . oh. Uh-oh.'

Sally's voice suddenly trailed off.

Slowly, nursing my arm, I stood up from behind the cabinet and one by one, the others followed.

Professor Maxwell Wally shrieked and staggered backwards. In his hand, he held a long, white . . . dinosaur bone.

Which he dropped. Quite suddenly. From the shock.

CRASH!

Six pairs of horrified eyes looked down at the floor. A priceless bone from the world's only complete Ockersaurus skeleton lay smashed to smithereens.

'Oops,' said Sally Champion.

Chapter Eight

Did I say my parents were a pair of old softies? Let me correct that. Up on the roof, before we got caught, I *thought* they were a pair of old softies.

But when Professor Wally woke them at midnight to tell them we'd broken into the museum, that suddenly changed.

That's the precise moment they stopped being old softies, and became a pair of two-headed, fire-breathing, baby-eating ogres on the warpath.

The drive back from the museum was a nightmare. First, Dad yelled and Mum cried. Then Mum yelled and Dad sat there with so much steam coming out of his ears that the windows fogged up and he had to turn the demister on. The yelling and crying went on all the way to the twenty-four-hour Accident and Emergency section of the Blue Rock Hospital where I was going to have my arm x-rayed.

'We're not angry,' Mum kept saying, sobbing hysterically. 'Just disappointed . . .'

'Speak for yourself!' shouted Dad. 'I'm not only angry, I'm *furious*!'

Everybody seemed to have forgotten I was mortally wounded and in danger of dying in the back seat.

'Dad, I think I've broken my arm,' I reminded him.

'Thank you, you saved me the trouble!' snapped Dad unsympathetically.

'Nick!' said Mum, shocked but starting to laugh.

I tried another approach. 'We weren't purposely breaking the law . . . we were working on a story for the newspaper . . .'

'THAT — NEWSPAPER!' roared Dad. 'Don't even mention — THAT — NEWSPAPER!' And he was off again.

I sat there with Scoop dripping water all over my feet, watching the windscreen wipers and wondering how the others were going with their parents.

I reckoned that with my arm in plaster, I had a good chance of getting off school for a few days as well as missing out on the lecture that was bound to follow the museum incident.

Wrong!

The next morning Mum woke me up and told me to get dressed. Jasper and Dad were already in the car. I knew something serious was up because Dad had taken the day off work, and usually Jasper and I walked to school. Normally being driven was a treat. But I had the feeling this was no treat. The radio, which was usually tuned to Mum's favourite station Dag-FM, was silent. So was everybody else. Besides, we were heading in the opposite direction to school.

'Where are we going?' I asked meekly.

'To the museum,' said Mum, staring straight ahead. 'To discuss things.'

By the time we got to the dinosaur room, there was quite a crowd gathered. I saw Miss Weinburger, the crusty old school principal, and my heart sank. This wasn't a good sign. Mrs Bottomley was there too, wearing her purple tea cosy on her head and blowing her nose on her white lace hanky. Standing next to her was — gulp — Professor Wally. A short distance away, I saw Mr and Mrs Champion talking quietly to Mrs Halliday, Frankie's mum. Sally and Frankie were standing silently beside them.

'It's all her fault,' whispered Jasper, pointing at

Sally. 'If she hadn't been showing off, jumping out at Professor Wally the way she did, none of this would have happened.'

I said nothing. After all, we were the ones who'd egged Sally on to prove how brave she was. And how was she to know that the giant shadow belonged to tiny little Professor Wally? None of us had realised that when a light shines at somebody from below them — like the spotlights surrounding the Ockersaurus — it throws a much larger shadow than normal.

Just as we arrived, Toby and his dad rushed through the door after us. Mr Trotter's shirt was on inside-out, his tie was skewwhiff — as usual he looked like he'd just been caught in a tornado.

'Half the town's here,' I muttered to Jasper.

'Haven't you ever heard of a public execution?' she whispered back.

'Good. We're all here.' Mrs Bottomley nodded primly at Mr Trotter and motioned everyone to gather around. 'I've called you all together to discuss the very disturbing events which took place here last night . . .'

'We can explain it all, Mrs Bottomley,' interrupted Sally. 'You see, Toby noticed that some of Neville's — I mean the Ockersaurus's — bones were missing, and we thought somebody was stealing them and . . .'

'Quiet!' Miss Weinburger pointed a bony finger at Sally and shook it fiercely.

Mrs Bottomley clicked her tongue. 'How preposterous! Nobody was stealing bones. I gave the professor permission to examine them for a special study he's doing. Now, it appears the children broke in and vandalised the museum . . .'

'We didn't vandalise it!' I objected. 'We had to cut the towel up to make a sling for my arm . . .'

Mrs Bottomley gave me a look that made the words freeze in my mouth. Then she blew her nose as loudly as a foghorn, making everyone jump.

'Fortunately, the towel was the only piece of property damaged,' she said coldly, stuffing the hanky into the sleeve of her jumper.

I thought guiltily of the dinosaur bone, smashed to smithereens on the floor. Didn't Mrs Bottomley know about that? Maybe the professor had forgotten to tell her.

'But it could have been much worse. A gang of children, rampaging through our precious exhibits . . . they could have broken something . . .'

'Now, just hang on a minute.' Mr Trotter gave Mrs Bottomley one of his lopsided smiles. 'The kids didn't mean any harm. Surely an explanation and an apology would fix things up?'

The Champions nodded in agreement. 'Our

Sally's a good girl. Why not let them off this time with a warning?'

Professor Wally gave an outraged squeak. 'A warning? They nearly scared the living daylights out of me.'

I shifted uncomfortably, waiting for him to break the news about the dinosaur bone. But before he could say anything else, Mrs Bottomley jumped in.

'If Professor Wally wasn't such a kind-hearted man he would have called the police in.' She patted her purple curls and smiled shyly at him. 'As it is, he's been generous enough to offer to forget the whole incident as long as the children don't step foot inside this museum until he returns to the United States.'

And that wasn't all. 'I'm strongly considering whether to suspend the lot of them,' added Miss Weinburger grumpily. 'Giving the school a bad name . . .'

'Oh, I'm sure that's not necessary,' said Mrs Halliday hastily. 'The children have all learned a lesson from this — and they're all terribly sorry about it. Aren't you Francesca?'

Frankie nodded. 'On behalf of all of us I'd like to apologise for all the trouble we've caused, and also for thinking that Professor Wally was a dinosaur bone thief.'

The professor stroked his little pointy beard and looked wounded.

'. . . and we're especially sorry that we made him drop the dinosaur bone and break it,' she concluded.

'WHAT!' Mrs Bottomley looked at the professor, aghast. 'You never said anything about a broken bone!'

'No, no, Ma'am,' said the professor hurriedly, rushing forward to steady her. 'The child is mistaken. She was talking about the *boy's* bone that was broken.'

'No, she wasn't,' said Jasper. 'She's talking about that dinosaur bone. We frightened you and you dropped it and it smashed on the floor, remember?'

Mrs Bottomley shrieked, and tottered backwards on her high heels as if she were about to faint. 'Oh, good lord . . . this is an international scandal . . . if this gets out I'll be sacked . . .'

Professor Wally patted her arm reassuringly. 'Calm yourself, dear lady. The children are lying.' He glared at us. 'The bones are fossilised, at any rate. They're as hard as rock. You couldn't break them even if you wanted to.'

I stared at the professor, totally confused. Why was he lying about the dinosaur bone? After all, it was our fault that he'd dropped it. And we'd all seen it happen.

The grown-ups looked at each other uncertainly.

'Come. See for yourself,' said the professor smoothly.

He took Mrs Bottomley's arm and led her over to the Ockersaurus. The rest of us trooped over behind them. As I stood before the dinosaur, I felt something gritty under my shoe. It looked like some sort of white powder. Maybe it was tiny fragments of bone, left behind when it smashed. Because the bone *had* smashed. Sally nudged me and pointed. She'd noticed the white powder, too.

'You see?' The professor pointed to the dinosaur with a flourish. 'Perfectly intact!'

I looked at the Ockersaurus. I counted the rib bones. I checked his feet. Then I rubbed my eyes, and looked again.

Every single bone was in its place. And not one of them was broken.

'I don't understand it.' Toby sighed deeply. 'I'm completely stumped.'

'Join the club,' I said moodily, staring out of the window of the Cave. I'd been mulling over the morning's events all day at school and I still hadn't come any closer to an answer. The professor had lied; we had no doubt about that. But why? And what had happened to the broken bone?

'I think we should forget about it,' said Jasper. 'After all, that was the bargain we made. And we did get off pretty lightly, considering.'

I shuddered, remembering how close we'd come to having *Street Wise* banned forever. That's what all the grown-ups had wanted. If it wasn't for Mr Trotter making a brilliant speech about the freedom of the press, the newspaper would have been scrapped. As it was, we were now under tight controls. Our parents had to approve every single story before we started investigating it. That way, they said, they could make sure we'd stay out of trouble.

The only problem was, knowing parents, they'd want us to stick to stories about school fêtes and lost kittens. It was a disaster whichever way you looked at it. Not only had we failed in the Spooking Sally Challenge, we'd made complete idiots of ourselves chasing a story about a non-existent dinosaur thief.

The only good thing to come out of it was the plaster cast on my arm. Getting kids to sign it was the only thing I had to look forward to in my whole life. I cheered up slightly. I could do that tomorrow.

'It looks like we're back to square one with *Street Wise*,' said Toby gloomily. 'No lead story and a lot of space to fill. Do you think Porky Merron's warts would make a front page story, Hugo?'

'I could try and beat it up a bit,' I said doubtfully. 'That's if our parents approve, of course.'

'How about Jasper's celebrity interview with the professor?' Frankie suggested. 'If we put that on the front page, he and Mrs Bottomley might not be quite as angry with us.'

'Sounds like sucking up to me,' I said. Not only that, we'd really gone off the professor since he lied about the broken bone. He'd obviously patched it up somehow so he wouldn't get into trouble with Mrs Bottomley. But now everybody thought *we* were the liars. It just wasn't fair.

Toby grimaced. 'Still, it's worth a try. It looks like we've made a mistake and the best thing we can do is admit it.'

Frankie's face fell. 'Uh-oh. I just remembered. I never got around to taking his photograph. There's no way he'll let me take it now.'

Toby thought for a moment, then snapped his fingers at Myron, the computer.

'Problem solved. We'll get it off the Internet. He's a famous professor — his university will have a picture of him for sure. We'll download it to Myron and print it out.'

Jasper checked her notes as Toby tapped into the Net. 'It's the University of Chicago. He's head of the Natural History Department.'

I went back to staring out the window. It was all my fault, really. If I hadn't promised Sally Champion a job on *Street Wise*, we would never have broken into the museum to try to scare her, and we wouldn't have been caught and . . .

'Hey!' Toby's puzzled cry woke me up out of my daydream. 'Look at this!'

We crowded around the computer. The screen was full of small square photographs of people, under the heading 'Faculty — University of Chicago'.

'Where's Professor Wally? Is he there?' Jasper pushed her way to the front and stood breathing down Toby's neck.

Toby tapped the screen. 'He's there all right.'

I craned my neck. Toby was pointing at a picture of a man with a small pointy beard. Underneath, it said, *'Prof. Maxwell Wally, Head of Natural History'*.

But something was wrong. Apart from the beard, he didn't look anything like Professor Wally. He was older for a start, and a lot fatter. The more I looked, the more convinced I was — I'd never seen that man before in my life.

'That's not Professor Wally,' said Jasper, exasperated. 'They've made a mistake. They've used the wrong picture.'

'Maybe not.' Toby blinked at us through his thick spectacles. There was a long silence.

'What do you mean, maybe not?' asked Frankie.

Toby shrugged. 'Maybe this man on the screen here *is* Professor Wally.'

'What are you talking about, Toby? We've never seen that man before. If that's Professor Wally, then . . .'

The realisation hit me like a ten-tonne rock.

Toby nodded slowly.

'Precisely, Hugo. If that's the real Professor Wally . . . then who is the man at the Blue Rock Museum?'

Chapter Nine

Nobody said a word. Finally, Frankie spoke. 'What are you saying — that Professor Wally is an impostor?'

Toby shrugged. 'It depends which Professor Wally you're talking about. The man *we* know as Professor Wally doesn't look anything like the Professor Wally who works at the University of Chicago.' Toby blinked at us stubbornly. 'First, he lies about breaking the bone. Then, this. It's all a bit odd, don't you think?'

Jasper snorted impatiently. 'Why would somebody go to the trouble of coming all the way to Australia to impersonate some crusty old professor?'

My mind was reeling. We'd already made fools of ourselves by accusing the professor of being a dinosaur bone thief. What if Toby was wrong again? Professor Wally would probably go straight to the police this time — and that would definitely be the end of *Street Wise*. 'Maybe Jasper's right,' I said anxiously. 'Maybe the university used the wrong picture.'

Toby nodded. 'It's possible. There's one easy way to find out.' He sat down at the computer again and started tapping away. 'We'll E-mail the university. Find out where he is.'

I watched as Toby typed a message on the screen.

I've found some old bones in my backyard and they look a bit prehistoric. I need to contact Professor Maxwell Wally urgently to discuss them. Can you please tell me where I can find him? Signed, Professor Toby Trotter, Esq.

As he zapped it off to the other side of the world, I scratched Scoop behind the ears while I thought. If the university replied to our E-mail and told us Professor Wally was in Blue Rock studying the Ockersaurus, then we knew Toby's theory was wrong. On the other hand, if they said he was in Chicago . . . I checked my watch. It was late at night in Chicago. Unless somebody was working back, we probably wouldn't get a reply until tomorrow.

Just then, I heard the unmistakable sound of a skateboard hurtling down the concrete path towards the Cave.

Sally Champion! With all the trouble we were in, I'd almost forgotten about her. The Spooking Sally Challenge seemed like something we'd done a million years ago.

Toby sighed. 'She's come to claim her prize, I suppose. And nobody could say she doesn't deserve it. She well and truly proved she isn't afraid of anything.'

'And got us into a whole heap of trouble in the process,' added Jasper crossly.

'I think we should look on the bright side,' suggested Frankie. 'After all, we were starting to run out of ideas for the newspaper. Having a new person might spark things up a bit!'

'Hmmph.' Jasper didn't look convinced. 'Well, there's nothing we can do about it, so we may as well accept it . . .'

I watched the door expectantly, waiting for Sally to burst through. Instead, there was a timid knock.

'Are you sure it's Sally?' Jasper sounded as puzzled as I was.

I opened the door with my good arm. Sally stood there, dressed in her cowgirl outfit, with her skateboard tucked under her arm. She smiled, but it was a small smile. Too small to see her pink and green braces. A no-braces smile.

'Hi. Can I come in?'

It wasn't like Sally to ask permission. Usually she barged in chattering at the top of her voice, helped herself to whatever food was available, and did a belly flop onto the nearest couch.

'Is something wrong?' asked Frankie.

Sally shook her head.

'Nothing's wrong. I just came to forfeit the Challenge. And to apologise.'

Forfeit the Challenge? My jaw dropped. 'But ... but you won ...'

'Are you telling us you don't want the job on *Street Wise*? After all this fuss?' Jasper said.

Jasper didn't sound half as happy as I thought she would. Some people, I thought, are just impossible to please.

Sally stood there awkwardly. 'I feel really bad about what happened at the museum. It's my fault we got caught. It's my fault that you can't write the stories you want to for your newspaper.' She pointed at my plaster cast. 'And in a way, it's my fault Hugo broke his arm.'

'It's not like you did it on purpose, Sally,' said Frankie kindly.

Toby nodded. 'It's the risk you take when you're

investigating a big story. Nobody blames you, Sally. It was just as much my fault for chasing the story in the first place.'

'And luckily I was there to save Hugo's life,' boasted Jasper. 'Sister Meryl at the hospital said my sling was just as good as a real one.'

But Sally wouldn't listen. She was convinced the whole thing was her fault, and she told us she wanted to make up for it. First, by forfeiting the Challenge. And secondly, by helping us to clear our name so that *Street Wise* could go back to the way it was.

'What do you mean, clear our name?' I said. 'We were wrong. We've admitted it.'

Sally reached into her pocket and pulled out a small plastic bag. Inside, there was a tiny amount of something that looked like white powder.

'Here. You're the crime reporter, aren't you? I swept this up this morning with my detective kit when the grown-ups weren't watching.' She handed it to me. 'It was on the floor, exactly where Professor Wally dropped that bone and broke it.'

Toby nodded approvingly. 'Good work, Sally.'

Sally put her hands on her hips and stared at us with a hint of her old confidence. 'You can't tell me something isn't fishy. Why did the professor lie about the broken bone? And how come it wasn't broken when we went back to the museum this morning?'

Toby snapped his fingers. 'That's exactly what I've been saying, Sally — but you're just about the only person who agrees with me.' Quickly, he filled her in on the Internet photograph.

'So there are plenty of unanswered questions,' he concluded. 'But no hard evidence.'

Sally's eyes were shining. She pointed at the small plastic bag I was still holding in my hand. 'That might be a good start.'

'Any idea what it is?'

Sally shook her head. 'I thought it might be flour at first. We have it all over the floor in the bakery. But I tasted a little bit, and it's definitely not.'

I stared hard at the powder in the bag. Something — a memory, perhaps — tickled the edge of my brain just out of reach. Where had I seen powder like that?

'Is it talcum powder?' I opened the bag and sniffed it, answering my own question. 'Nope.' But again, there was something familiar about it — a faint, chalky odour that I knew I'd smelled before.

I slipped the bag in my pocket. Maybe it would come to me later.

Toby thumped his fist on the desk in frustration. 'If only we could go back to the museum to investigate. We can't solve a mystery with just one clue!'

'Don't even think about it,' warned Jasper. 'They'll close down *Street Wise* altogether if you get

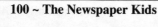

caught. Besides, how can you be so sure it *is* a mystery? We've got no proof of anything.'

Just then, the computer beeped. The E-mail icon — a pigeon with a note tied to its foot — was flying across the screen. That meant somebody had sent a message. The five of us looked at each other. Somebody from . . . Chicago?

We watched impatiently as Toby grabbed the mouse and clicked on the pigeon.

'Well? Is it from the university? What does it say? Is the professor in Blue Rock?' The clamour of excited voices filled the Cave, but Toby didn't even seem to hear.

Unable to bear the suspense, I peered over his shoulder.

> Dear Professor Trotter,

I read out loud.

> I was just about to close the office when I got your message. I regret to inform you that Professor Wally is unable to be reached at the moment as he is . . .

Oh, crikey!

> . . . as he is out of the country working on a special study.

I stopped reading, filled with disappointment. So Toby was wrong again. Professor Maxwell Wally was working at Blue Rock Museum just as he was supposed to be.

'Read the rest of the message, Hugo,' Toby said quietly. 'You didn't finish it.'

> The professor is currently in Iceland . . .

I stopped, bewildered.

> The professor is currently in Iceland studying the remains of a ten thousand year old woman which were found perfectly preserved in a glacier,

Toby continued triumphantly.

> We do not expect him back in Chicago for another ten days.

He spun around on his chair to face us. 'There! The real Professor Wally is in Iceland. Is that enough of a mystery for you?'

'I'm going back to the museum.' Sally made for the door.

'Don't! We can't risk it!' Jasper, panicking, grabbed her arm. 'They'll close *Street Wise* . . .'

'I've got nothing to do with *Street Wise* any more — remember?' said Sally, shaking her off. 'This is my own detective work. If I'm caught, I'll say you had nothing to do with it.'

The words of the E-mail message kept running

around in my brain.

'The professor is in Iceland . . . we do not expect him back in Chicago for ten days . . .'

Who was the man posing as Professor Wally and why was he so interested in the bones of the Ockersaurus?

My reporter's instinct told me this could be a huge story, but one thing was certain — without Sally's help, we might never know the answers.

Toby leaned against the desk, looking perplexed. 'Why are you doing this for us?'

Sally grinned, showing her braces for the first time that day.

'Because I got you into this mess. And I'm going to get you out of it.'

Then she jumped on her skateboard, and was gone.

By the time I got to school the next morning I was ready to explode with curiosity.

'Meet me under the old tree at the back of the school at morning break,' said the note Sally passed to me during Maths. I caught her eye and nodded. Good, she must have some information for us.

As soon as the bell rang, Frankie ran to get Jasper and Toby, and I wandered over to the tree mulling over the events of the past twenty-four hours.

The old trunk was knotted and gnarled, and covered with initials and love-hearts. School kids had been scratching their name into that tree for sixty years. I started to search for my Great-aunt Miranda's initials, but before I had a chance to find them, the others arrived.

'We've only got ten minutes, so I'll get straight to the point,' said Sally breathlessly, checking over her shoulder to make sure we were alone.

Quickly, she filled us in.

'After I left the Cave, I rode straight to the museum. It was four-thirty, so it was still open,' she said. 'But because we'd promised not to step foot in the museum again, I decided to do my investigation from the outside — by looking in the windows.'

Taking cover in the bushes, Sally told us, she worked her way around the museum until she found Professor Wally's office.

'Well? Was he in there?' demanded Jasper eagerly.

Sally nodded. 'He was busy working on something but I couldn't see exactly what it was because there was a filing cabinet in the way. But when he stepped back, I noticed that his hands were covered in white powder.'

My heart thumped. 'Like the stuff in the packet?'

Sally shrugged. 'Maybe. It was on his shoes as well. Whatever it was, he'd got it all over himself. I watched him for about an hour, trying to figure out what he was doing. Finally, he stepped back and held up two bones to the light.'

'Two bones?' asked Toby excitedly. 'What did they look like?'

Sally wrinkled her forehead. 'Quite short, and curved, with a pointed end — like the blade of a pirate's dagger. They were identical. He left the room with them and he was smiling.'

She took a deep breath and continued. 'I knew I had to keep track of him, so I kept my head low and crept around the entire building looking in the windows. I finally located him in the dinosaur room.'

'And?' I was feeling sick with suspense.

'By the time I got there, he was re-attaching a bone to the Ockersaurus. It was the very tip of the tail. That accounted for the dagger shape.'

Sally looked at us and spread her arms wide. 'Then he got his briefcase from his office and went home. That's all I can tell you.'

'Oh.' I couldn't hide my disappointment. 'So he was studying the bones and then putting them back — just like Mrs Bottomley said.'

I butted my forehead against the old tree in frustration. Despite Sally's efforts, we were still none the wiser; still no closer to finding out what had happened to the broken bone or what the mysterious white powder was. The whole thing seemed hopeless.

'Just a minute,' said Toby slowly. 'You said there were two bones, Sally. What happened to the other one?'

Sally shrugged again. 'Search me. I suppose he put it back on the dinosaur before I got to the window.'

'But you said it was the tip of the tail bone,' said Toby urgently. 'There's only one of those. Why would he have two? Two identical tail bones, when there is only one Ockersaurus?'

He was right.

As the five of us stared at each other wide-eyed, the bell rang.

'Darn it,' groaned Toby. 'We'll have to continue this at lunch time.'

As we walked back up to the classroom, Sally tapped my cast. 'I'll have to sign it while there's still room left on it,' she said. 'Or maybe I can carve my initials into it, like that old tree!'

I laughed. 'No way! The whole thing would fall apart. Look, it's already going a bit crumbly around the edges.' I scraped the end of the cast with my fingernail, and watched as a miniature shower of dry plaster splattered on the ground.

Then I stopped.

I looked at the grains of white plaster on the

ground. I thought of the mysterious white powder. *'Two bones,'* Sally had said. *'They were identical . . .'*

'What's wrong, Hugo?' Frankie shoved me from behind. 'Come on, we're going to be late for Art.'

I grabbed the bag of white powder from my pocket and smelled it. Dry, dusty, chalky. Just like the smell of . . . the plaster room at the hospital.

The penny dropped.

'Come on!' I grabbed Sally and Frankie and pulled them away from the classroom door. 'I'm going to the museum, and I need some witnesses!'

'*YOU* again!'

Mrs Bottomley gave an outraged shriek and started chasing after us. 'Come here this instant or I'll call the police! I'll call Miss Weinburger! I'll . . . I'll . . .' She gave a giant sneeze that nearly blew her backwards. 'Oh, this wretched hayfever!'

'You'd better know what you're doing, Hugo,' muttered Frankie, as the three of us sprinted down the hallway towards the dinosaur room.

'Just have your camera ready,' I panted. 'And keep your fingers crossed.'

'Vandals!' screamed Mrs Bottomley, trotting after us like a fat angry poodle. 'Security! Help!'

I heard Sally whooping with glee as she threw her skateboard onto the smooth lino floor. 'Jump on!'

She grabbed Frankie and me, and before I knew it, the three of us were zooming down the corridor with people scattering left, right and centre.

As usual, there was quite a crowd in front of the Ockersaurus — but when they saw the skateboard coming they jumped out of the way quick smart.

'Hey! What's the big idea!' said a woman angrily. 'Wait your turn!'

I heard Mrs Bottomley turn the corner still yelling for the security guard. Any minute now she'd crash tackle us to the ground. It was now or never.

Leaping off the skateboard, I high jumped over the white rope towards the Ockersaurus. As I crossed the red laser beam, the alarm went off. The sound of a wailing siren and clanging bells was deafening.

Flustered by the noise, I stumbled towards the dinosaur, my hand outstretched and grabbed the bone at the very tip of the tail.

Above the terrifying shriek of the alarm, I heard Mrs Bottomley scream. As the crowd of people in front of me gasped in horror, I snapped the bone in two.

A small shower of plaster fell pitter-patter onto the floor.

Chapter Ten

'See? She's perfectly harmless. Behind the glass, there's no way she can possibly touch you.'

I peeked nervously between my fingers. Amelia the Huntsman sat on a rock inside the old aquarium and stared impassively at me.

Sally stroked the glass softly. 'Isn't she pretty? I'll be so sad to say goodbye to her, but it's time she returned to the wild.'

I grimaced. Pretty wasn't the word I would have used to describe Amelia. Maybe in the spider world she'd qualify as a movie star, but by human standards? Ugghh. Still, at least I could look at Amelia now without turning into a quivering heap of jelly.

It was three weeks after Sally had agreed to help me lose my fear of spiders, and I was doing well. Sally called these daily eyeball sessions, 'facing my fear'.

'Gradual exposure to the object of fear has been scientifically proven to cure phobias,' Sally reminded me. 'Now, are you ready for the final test?'

I eyed Amelia again and weighed up the pros and cons. If I did it, I was almost guaranteed to lose my fear of spiders forever. Maybe I'd never really like them the way Sally did — but at least I wouldn't be constantly jumping out of my skin every time I saw a leaf move.

I made my decision. 'Okay. I'm ready.'

I closed my eyes and took ten deep breaths. My heart started pumping but I willed it to slow down.

'Go,' said Sally.

I opened my eyes, aimed for the aquarium — then pressed my face so hard against the glass that I could hardly breathe.

I stared at Amelia, only millimetres away. Her black beady eyes stared back at me. She waved a hairy leg at me; I didn't flinch.

CLICK! Frankie took a photo.

'Bravo!' said Sally. 'You've done it!'

So that was how I beat my fear of spiders.

Frankie's photo of me and Amelia made the front

page of the next issue of *Street Wise*. The one *after* we exposed the fake professor. That issue sold out quickly and we had to print another fifty copies, just to send to the real Professor Wally in America. So much for our circulation problems.

'BONE SWAP SCANDAL!' screamed the headline that Toby put over my story. 'IMPOSTOR NABBED SWIPING FAMOUS OCKERSAURUS!'

You see, Toby had been right all along — even if the only person who believed him from the start was Sally.

'Well, you had a lot to do with it, Hugo,' Toby insisted modestly. 'After all, if you hadn't realised the fake professor was making plaster copies of the bones, he would have got away with it.'

He nearly did. By the time the police arrived at the museum, the phoney professor had fled town. They caught him at the airport with a suitcase full of Ockersaurus bones. When Mrs Bottomley checked Neville, she nearly fainted with the shock. All of the bones were fakes — he'd quietly worked his way from one end of the Ockersaurus to the other. The whole time he was working late supposedly 'studying' the bones one by one, he'd been making copies of them and replacing them.

As I explained in my exclusive report, the phoney professor's real name was Freddy Sharp. He was one of Professor Wally's assistants at the university —

that's how he knew the real professor was going to be away for a long time studying the Glacier Woman in Iceland. He also knew how much money the Ockersaurus bones were worth on the black market, and he reckoned he had a foolproof way to steal them so that nobody would know.

Mrs Bottomley was devastated. But the funny thing was, after Freddy Sharp left, Mrs Bottomley never had hayfever again. It was all that plaster dust floating about the museum that was making her sneeze.

'Poor old Bottoms,' said Jasper. 'She'll have to find another boyfriend. But this time, she'd better make sure he's who he says he is!'

Luckily, Mrs Bottomley didn't blame us. In fact, once her broken heart mended, she summonsed all of us to the museum — along with our parents and Miss Weinberger — to formally apologise for calling us vandals and liars.

'You children have saved one of Blue Rock's greatest natural treasures,' she trilled fondly. 'Not to mention my job,' I heard her mutter under her breath.

After that, our parents could hardly keep punishing us, could they? They had to admit that when it came to breaking big news stories, we knew what we were doing. So they left us alone, and *Street Wise* went back to normal.

Well, almost.

Two days after Freddy Sharp was arrested, Toby called a special meeting at the Cave and invited Sally to be there.

'Sally Champion, on behalf of the entire staff of *Street Wise*, I would like to offer you a job as honorary reporter,' he said solemnly.

For once in her life, Sally was lost for words.

'Say yes, Sally,' begged Frankie. 'After all, you did win the Challenge fair and square.'

'Go on!' I urged. 'If it wasn't for you making us go into the museum that night when we were all so scared, we would never have seen the broken bone — and we would never have got our front page story.'

'I would never have got over my fear of the dark,' added Toby.

'And me, my fear of heights!' said Frankie.

I dug Jasper in the arm.

'Oh, all right,' she said huffily, flicking her plaits. 'I admit I wasn't too keen on the idea at first . . .' She stuck out her hand for Sally to shake and grinned. 'But I must say, Sally Champion, it's grown on me.'

So Sally joined *Street Wise*. Her parents agreed, as long as she still helped out at the bakery two afternoons a week, and Saturday morning.

It seemed the only person who wasn't happy about *Street Wise* saving the dinosaur was Marilyn Miller, the TV reporter with yellow hair and bushy black eyebrows. She had to interview us for the news, and boy, was she stroppy.

But the best thing that happened was the letter that arrived one month later. By then, we were hard at work on the next issue of *Street Wise*, and we'd almost forgotten about Freddy Sharp and the disappearing dinosaur bones.

It was Mum who opened it.

'The Mayor of Blue Rock cordially invites you and your family to be present at a special ceremony,' she read out loud, 'to honour the reporters of *Street Wise* who stopped the theft of the world's rarest dinosaur. The town wishes to present them with . . . *bravery awards*!'

'And to present the awards, all the way from Chicago . . . the real Professor Maxwell Wally!'

There was a big drum roll, and the town hall erupted with applause. A large man with a pointy beard and small spectacles walked onto the stage, waving jovially.

'Ladies and gentleman, I assure you I really *am* Professor Wally,' he joked, waving something in the air. 'I've got my driver's licence here if anybody would like to check it.'

The crowd laughed and clapped.

'Are you ready, Sally?' asked Toby. 'Got your notes?'

Sally's spurs jangled as she jumped from one foot to the other with excitement. 'You bet! But are you sure you want me to make the acceptance speech?'

The rest of us looked at each other and nodded. If it wasn't for Sally, we wouldn't even be getting the awards. This was her honour.

'. . . and to accept the awards on behalf of the *Street Wise* newspaper kids, I am very pleased to introduce their newest reporter MISS — SALLY — CHAMPION!' The professor turned to us and beamed broadly as the crowd broke out into thunderous applause.

Sally walked confidently over to the professor, took the awards and shook his hand.

Then she turned to face the audience. The town hall was packed. Six hundred and fifty people gazed expectantly at Sally, waiting for her to speak. Six hundred and fifty pairs of eyes focused entirely on her.

Sally opened her mouth, but no sound came out.

She swallowed. Then she stammered.

Then all of a sudden, in front of six hundred and fifty people, Sally's knees buckled and she fell on the ground in a dead faint.

That's how we found out the one thing that spooks Sally Champion. Public speaking!

The Newspaper Kids 1

★ **Blue Rock
Kid Power**

by Juanita Phillips

Jasper nearly kills Toby on the skate ramp,
then the Mayor decides to close the park.
Everyone in Blue Rock is blaming the kids.
Toby is the only person who knows the real
story and it's a story that *must* be told! But
making headlines and digging up secrets is
a dangerous business. Someone doesn't want
the newspaper to hit the streets and it looks
like they'll do anything to stop it.

If a story breaks, the newspaper kids are on
the case.

The Newspaper Kids 2

✱ Mandy Miami and the Miracle Motel

by Juanita Phillips

War has been declared!
Howard Fitzherbert has started his own
newspaper to try and run the newspaper kids
out of business! He's stealing all their ideas.
They need a special front page story. Toby's
favourite singer, Mandy Miami, could be
exactly what they want, but Mandy is so
mysterious, even her fan club don't know
how to find her. The World Wide Web holds
the clues but the newspaper kids aren't the
only ones surfing the Net – so is the Shark.

If a story breaks, the newspaper kids are
on the case!

The
Newspaper
Kids 3

✳ Pegleg Paddy's Puppy Factory

by Juanita Phillips

Jasper and Hugo are trapped at Auntie Marge's Fun Camp for Kids – but the only ones having fun are mean old Auntie Marge and her no-good son, Pegleg Paddy. Their creepy old house is full of strange goings-on that have the newspaper kids' noses twitching. With the help of a little lost dog, they are soon on the trail of the biggest dog-gone story their newspaper has ever published.

If a story breaks, the newspaper kids are on the case!

Order Form

To order direct from the publishers, just make a list of the titles you want and fill in the form below:

Name ....

Address ....

....

....

Send to: Dept 6, HarperCollins Publishers Ltd, Westerhill Road, Bishopbriggs, Glasgow G64 2QT.

Please enclose a cheque or postal order to the value of the cover price, plus:

UK & BFPO: Add £1.00 for the first book, and 25p per copy for each additional book ordered.

Overseas and Eire: Add £2.95 service charge. Books will be sent by surface mail but quotes for airmail despatch will be given on request.

A 24-hour telephone ordering service is available to holders of Visa, MasterCard, Amex or Switch cards on 0141- 772 2281.

Collins
An *Imprint* of HarperCollins*Publishers*